I0664861

Greater Spirits

The River Sanctuary Series, Volume 3

Zabe Truesdell

Published by Zabe Truesdell, 2018.

This is a work of fiction. Similarities to real people, places, or events are entirely coincidental.

GREATER SPIRITS

First edition. July 31, 2018.

Written by Zabe Truesdell.

Big Thank You to all of the same folks who have helped me in the past and continue to do so.

Thanks to Charlie and Carol for their work in helping with edits.

A big thank you to all of the many fans who have given me such warm feedback on the prior books and for their insistence that I get this book to them. I hope you enjoy it as much as I have.

And finally, to those fans who crossed into their own Sanctuary before this book was finished, you are greatly missed.

Chapter 1

"*There is no death, only a change of worlds.*"
    -*Chief Seattle*

Of all the incarnations of hell Thomas Salazar had faced since death, this one was by far the most disturbing. He sat in the middle seat of a large 747 plane. Snoring passengers, too large for their small seats, spilled over into his cramped personal space from either side. The seat in front of him leaned back far into his lap, lightly crushing his legs to the point where they would have lost all circulation if they still had blood flowing through them. Somewhere off in the distance, a baby screamed as the changing pressure crushed its delicate eardrums.

The lone TV in site buzzed with an annoying hum but showed no update. The temperature alternated in weird intervals between uncomfortably warm and ridiculously cold. The air smelled stale and unpleasant. It was a scene he had suffered through more than once in life, and some poor sod was now doomed to an eternity of it in death.

Or at least until Thomas and his group could find and free them.

"Cho? What's your status?"

"Not good, Friend Thomas." Thomas's second-in-command rang in his ear as if he had a Bluetooth radio. Given their connection, Thomas could have just extended himself through Cho's senses, but that felt like an immense violation. "I've made it to an aisle, but I'm trapped between two carts being pushed by people in uniforms. There is no room to go around, and every time I consider trying to dive through I either get interrupted by the ground shaking or someone stands and pulls down a storage hatch that blocks my path." His voice sounded more annoyed than Thomas remembered ever hearing. "Honestly, I am not even sure if I should be going forwards or backwards, but right now I am not moving either direction."

"I am in a cage." Buster's voice cut in, also laced with annoyance. "Bars are strong. Latch is out of reach. I will keep looking." The dog left off the part of being near frantic about realizing that he was, in a fashion, flying. Thomas knew the former Native American's feelings on that subject. Dogs belonged on the ground.

Thomas grunted as the seat on his legs suddenly moved forcefully from a kick. He looked up to find a six year old staring at him, obviously kicking the seat he stood in. The annoyance tested his patience to the point of snapping, when the child's face suddenly morphed into that of an Egyptian pharaoh. "Well, this is moving along nicely."

"Ug." Thomas groaned, looking away from his 'conscience'. "I think I preferred the brat."

"Yes, well, I told you this was a poor idea. Not all problems can be solved via 'plan a - beat everything into submission'. You lack the team to be able to complete this type of mission without... well... using all of your tools."

Thomas shook his head at Senebkay's near spoken suggestion. "No. I'm not giving you control, and we both know that me pulling in enough souls to make a difference would do just that."

Senebkay shrugged and kicked the seat once more. "Suit yourself. But without my help, your options are rather limited."

"Oh you could help. Maybe scout a little? Find the real souls?"

The ancient pharaoh shook his head and kicked the seat again. "No, I'm afraid I cannot do that. While the fact that you insist on keeping me in this quasi corporeal state of being has allowed me to possess this automaton, I suspect it's only because I continue to annoy you in the manner in which its designer intended it to do that its odd behavior has escaped notice. Were I to try and move about freely, I would no doubt encounter the same obstacles that your lesser souls have."

Thomas bristled at the term 'lesser souls'. Cohorts, friends, teammates, or other such terms were fine, but Thomas didn't like considering himself the leader of the group. He especially disliked the idea that he was, in truth, some kind of Greater Soul, superior to all of those who had agreed to join to him, capable of manipulating them in any way he saw fit if he truly desired it. It remained one of the primary reasons the idea of Senebkay regaining control frightened him. Nobody could predict what the pharoah might choose to do with the friends bound to him. To him, they were nothing more than slightly autonomous tools.

"Fine. Aside from giving you control, what would you suggest we do?"

The pharaoh looked about then grimaced. "Leave."

Thomas shook his head. "We can't leave. There's at least one soul here being punished with an eternity of this. Gods know how long he's been stuck in this... holding pattern. We need to find out who's doing this and stop them."

Senebkay shrugged. "You have no reader. No one who can examine the essence of this sanctuary and tell what's real and what's not."

"There has to be another way."

"Oh there is, but you will not like it, nor do I believe it is worth the risk of you trying. "

Thomas's options had long since been exhausted. He wanted to at least weigh everyone else's options before making a decision he knew he would be unhappy with. "What is it?"

The pharaoh sighed. "Link yourself to this Sanctuary, just as the rogue soul currently in control has done. That will put you on their radar."

"Would that work?"

The pharaoh shrugged. "Doubtful. You would have to contest the will of the rogue soul who already knows how this realm works. You would have to want to free this sanctuary far more than he or she wants to enslave it. Without pulling in your other souls, it is doubtful you have the willpower or fortitude to win that fight."

Thomas had dealt with enough rogue souls by now to suspect that Senebkay might actually be telling the truth on that. "And if I lose?"

"You and all those linked to you become tied to this realm, subject to the rules of the one in charge of it. This becomes your new normal, and unless someone else frees you you'll spend eternity in that seat."

Thomas growled, a low rumble that would have sounded more natural coming from Buster's throat. For all that he could be certain it might be Buster's response. Linking souls seemed to be giving him some of the traits of those whose memories he took on. "Abort. We'll meet back at Leo's plateau".

He did his best to disregard the smirk on Senebkay's face as he disappeared from the plane.

Chapter 2

Jacob shook his head, trying to wrap his mind around everything he heard. He wasn't sure it would be possible to do so. "This is fucking insane, you know that, right?"

"Aye mate. I know how this sounds."

Jacob didn't remember anything from the time that the funky warrior in the mini-skirt had challenged him. One minute he was charging the bastard, the next he stood in some tropical hut that apparently only existed in Jack's mind.

Oh, and Jack was apparently now the god of this bizarre land, and had used that power to rescue Jacob from whatever oblivion these ancient souls had consigned him to.

"So, you're Hades now. You've got all the power. What do you need me to do this for?"

Jack shook his head. "I've got a lot of power, aye, that's true. But not all of it lad. Not by a long shot." Jack waved his hand, creating a window that opened directly to a secluded beach where the waves were crashing violently on the shore. "These blokes, they were smart. Now that I'm on top, I can see how everything works. They aren't actually bound to me. They're bound to the helm I wear. The distinction is important."

"So you only get the power while wearing it?"

"Aye. But that's not the issue. The issue is that the line of connection to the object means that any member of the council can break their bond at any time they wish. They do that, and all of the souls bound through them get yanked from my control."

"Can't you just order them not to?"

Jack shrugged. "Not everyone at once. Might could get one or two before the others figured it out and revolted. Then we'd be stuck with a war I don't think we could win."

Jacob stared out to over the ocean for a bit himself, trying to take more of this in. "So instead you want me to start a war you don't know if you can win."

"Better odds." Jack noted with a shrug. "If there's anything I noted when I still lived, it's that people can be made to do most anything if they're scared enough. And with centuries of warfare in their recent memories, fear of 'the other' is ripe here. It won't take much to play up that fear to the point where even a minor misunderstanding will escalate."

"But why would you want to do that, man? You know how many people would die if this thing went full on battle again?"

"They're already dead, Jacob.."

"So am I. Doesn't mean I want to..."

Jack cut him off with a wave. "How much art have you seen since we got here, Jacob?"

The large black man considered for a moment. "None that I can think of. But I haven't exactly been looking."

"Well, I have. Much more so since taking the helm. There's none."

"Well, that's a bit weird but..."

"No songs. No advances in technology. Hell, even though they've gotten some knowledge from a hand full of souls that have been banished over here, there's no bloody advancements what so ever. These souls, they're stagnate, Jacob. A bloody pool of dead River stuff that cannot change. Even with me in charge, it's bloody unlikely that I could do much but make small alterations."

"So your plan's to kill everyone?"

"If it takes that, yes." Jack turned back and looked his friend in the eye. Jacob noted a gleam of seriousness he rarely saw, along with a tinge of something else... madness? "Listen lad. I know this sounds crazy. But you'll have to trust me on this. There's a chance I can get us home. If so, then all of these fair folk can be returned to the River, to be recycled as they should have been millennia ago. But I can't do that without a lot more power than we have. "

Jack turned back from the window and sat down on the edge of the bed, looking more exhausted than Jacob had seen him in a long time. "Trust me, lad. I've looked at this from many angles. I wouldn't be doing this if I could think of another way. But there's not. We do nothing and we're trapped here, like these souls are, till we all thin out so much that we're nothing but bloody automatons going through daily motions with no idea why we're doing it."

Jack sighed, a tinge of sadness entering his voice. "Many of the souls here have already reached that point. They're just bloody shells, mate. There's no true life left them. No dancing. No singing. It's all just a routine, most of which is set forth by the council to keep people going from one day to the next. Oblivion would be a blessing for them next to this."

Jacob shook his head. "I don't know man. Seems unfair, us playing god and all."

"There's no playing, Jacob. I am bloody god. At least here, anyway. But there's a reason they gave me the guise of Hades. I'm not the god of life. I'm the god of death. I can't do anything to bring joy to these souls. But I can end their misery. I can end their suffering. And maybe, just maybe, by doing so I can truly free us all."

Jacob still couldn't bring himself to fully buy into Jack's argument, no matter how much he wanted to trust his friend. But one of Jack's points rose above the rest as something he wanted desperately to believe. "So you really think you can get us home? How much power will it take?"

Jack sighed. "I don't know. Our links to our sanctuaries aren't actually gone. They're just very very faint. I can sense them with the power I've got now, but it's like trying to grab a rainbow. With enough power I could solidify it more, perhaps even use it to send us to the other side. Since it goes through the Glacier itself, there's even a chance that if I made it strong enough, we could bore a hole straight through and free everyone here."

"Great. I know you. You've played with this. You should have an idea of how much power this would take."

"A guess." Jack shrugged. "Not accurate. Potentially dangerous. But aye, I've a guess. We get half the souls here, I might can put someone on the other side. We get all the souls and I could probably break it down."

"All the souls in this realm or just on our side of the River?" Jacob knew the distinction could change just how difficult the outcome would prove.

"All the souls actually linked to Hades. I think that would be enough."

Jacob nodded. "So we don't actually have to start a holy war, just fake it enough to scare your new council into making you a true king."

"Aye and no." Jack said with a wave. "Aye, I could likely bring it down without a holy war. But doing so will weaken if not destroy me. Normally I'd not be concerned with that, small price to pay and all, but..."

Jacob knew exactly what Jack was leading to. "But that unleashes another god on the other side with small chance anyone could stop her."

"You've seen what's it's possible to do with that level of power here. Can ye imagine the damage she could do to the Prime?"

Jacob needed no more. "That can't be allowed to happen, Jack. Even if it means we stay here." The mere thought of that level of power being unleashed on the loved ones he left behind scared him more than he would admit.

"It won't lad. Even if I have to consign every last creature here to oblivion and put meself to sleep like some Elder God of Cthulhu, I'll not be letting this escape. But we have to try. This status quo is unacceptable."

"Fine." Jacob resigned himself to following his mentor into madness. "But you lose control of this, and I'll find a way to make you pay. Don't think I won't."

"Aye lad. I'd count on nothing less."

Chapter 3

Thomas stepped out onto Leo's plateau, the rest of his crew just behind him. He could feel the nearly spastic Italian suppress a moment of fear and disgust that the group would appear on the plateau and not at the base of it the way he had designed his sanctuary to work. It was rude, Thomas admitted, and in the not so recent past that would have encouraged him to not do it. Now it barely a passed as a thought. The Italian would get over it very quickly, he knew, and there was no time for games. There was only the job, and all of them had to make sacrifices for that.

Thomas merely wished that Leo would also sacrifice his "I told you so" style commentary.

"This job, I told you, you were not ready for it. Did you listen to me? No. And you did not succeed, did you?"

"No, Leo." Thomas raised his hand, but stopped short of actually pushing the Italian to silence through their link. "But it was a risk worth taking. If it had worked, we would have gotten much more power for the soul stone. "

"But it did not, so..."

"So we're pretty much where we would have been if we'd done nothing, aren't we? But we tried."

Leo's lecturing tone melted somewhat, replaced by a sense of concern. "I worry about you, Thomas. You take too much risk. One day, it may not work out so well."

Thomas knew even without the link that the Italian's concern was both genuine and well founded. There could be little helping it though. As he'd said many times, they all had to make sacrifices for the job, him more so than anyone. "I know, Leo. And I appreciate your concern. But we're in an arms race with someone who's had a century head start. We can't take the safe route here. Brother Coughlin could decide to take us out at any time."

"Or he might wait another century. Will it matter if you return yourself to the River? You must be smart about this."

The pharaoh stepped up, much less disturbing in his own body than he had been earlier when his face had taken over the child. "He has a point. There are better ways."

"Not you too." Thomas growled mentally, not wanting to appear even more insane than he felt by arguing with someone the rest of his crew still could not see. But the man's words carried some merit, more so because he could feel them echoed throughout all of the connections here. Cho and Buster wouldn't say it, feeling oddly that it was not their place to slow him down, even if he did put their souls at risk. They didn't need to say it, however, for him to sense it through their mutual links.

"Fine." Thomas said wearily with a sign. 'I'll try and slow it down a little." Thomas made himself a lawn chair and had a seat. He felt certain that Jack would have had a recliner and a beer in hand by now, but he decide that might be too much. Buster padded over and sat down at his side. Senebkay created himself a far too ornate gold throne and sat down at the edge of the group. Cho had already plopped into a lotus position near Leonardo's koi pond. If they hadn't been linked, Thomas wouldn't be certain the man was listening in. His link confirmed what he expected, that the man paid close attention to every word.

"What do you suggest, Leo?"

"Bring in assistance. Just as Jack brought you in and trained you, so should you be training new talent. People with the skills you do not have. "

"No." Thomas didn't even think about that option before rejecting it outright. "I know what you're thinking, Leo, and I can't fault your reasons. In most circumstances I would agree with you completely. But you more than anyone knows that if we did that, the only way we could trust them to not fall into Coughlin's hands would be for me to link to them. I don't want to do that anymore than I absolutely have to."

"Your reluctance is understandable, Thomas, but the team, it must be larger. We cannot..."

"It changes me, Leo." Thomas said in exasperation. He had been reluctant to fully admit his fear, even too himself, but now that he was being pushed, the reason was clear. "You may or may not have noticed, but I have. Every soul I take on changes me. It makes me something I wasn't. The changes are subtle, but noticeable. I've taken on small aspects of each of you since you joined with me. If I keep at this, how much longer will it be before there's no 'Thomas Salazar' left? How much longer before I become..."

"Me?" asked from his throne.

"...someone else entirely." Thomas finished for the benefit of those who couldn't hear the Pharaoh.

Leo walked over and placed a gentle hand on Thomas's shoulder. "Change, it is inevitable. Just as in life, we must embrace change in death or else why would we exist? Did you not pick up habits of your friends in life? I think, probably, you did. This is no different."

"It is different." Thomas sighed. But he knew he was losing this argument. He could feel it coming through all sides of the present links. Buster and Cho would still remain silent about it, but both agreed with Leo that their ranks were too small for the job they needed to do. Senebkay still found it ridiculous that Thomas wasn't binding himself to every soul that would listen. The complete and utter certainty coming in from all directions that he was wrong made it tough to trust his own decision.

Leo must have seen the internal struggle on Thomas's face. He chose to step back and see where it landed. Perhaps some feeling passed to him from the link they shared that he needed not push to win. Thomas shook his head and sighed.

"I don't like this."

"This, I am aware of." Leo replied with a hint of sympathy.

"Fine." Thomas relented. "If you can find a soul that will be willing to link to me then we'll train them. "

Leo smiled, though he attempted to suppress his instinctual excitement. "I know who to get in touch with. He is... not well liked... but he can do this job well."

"Fine." Thomas repeated. "In the mean time, find us another Sanctuary to free. This stone won't fill itself."

Chapter 4

"Please. Please, let me go. I'll do whatever you want!" The boy's voice cracked with a ragged tone. His clothes were already shredded from the whipping that the demons of his past had given him.

Brother Coughlin shook his head. "No." He felt for the boy. He really did. In all likelihood the boy's upbringing had lead him to dangerous beliefs. His moral compass would have been warped by a dogma difficult to resist. Difficult... but not impossible. "Did you really expect to escape judgment for your crimes? You murdered twenty-eight of your fellow humans. Your actions caused the death of six more. And you think that no price should be paid for this?"

"It was war. I was only trying to purge the unworthy."

"I have seen your soul, remember? What exactly were your inner thoughts during those dark times? How much joy did you take when you pulled the trigger? You knew it wrong. You had the chance to say no. But did you? No."

The boy prostrated himself. "Please. I would have been killed. You know that."

"Then you would have died a martyr. And your afterlife would have been truly glorious. Now...." He nodded to the demons, who brought their whiplashes down across the boy's back. "Now your eternity will be pain."

The boy continued his cries, but Coughlin cut his voice. This was justice, he knew, but he had little taste for it himself. Coughlin took the demons; created from the memories of those whose afterlife had been stained by the choices the boy had made, and tied them to Beelzebub.

Coughlin shuddered at the touch of the foul thing. Brother Giovanni had first proposed its creation many years ago as a buffer for the evil that Coughlin must link himself to. The saint had posited that, since souls had an affect on those who were taking them, directly controlling the amount of dark souls necessary to do their job would put him at risk of succumbing to their terrible influence.

By creating a buffer, Coughlin could still link to the power contained within, but not be directly influenced by it. Thus, they had created Beelzebub, so named for one of Satan's own, and poured all of those dark memories into it. Each time he freed a soul of its pain and anger, of its memories of being wronged, he poured those nightmares into this beast.

The result created a powerful embodiment of rage and angers whose single purpose was to visit suffering on those responsible for the memories that plagued it.

Its creativity stretched beyond any comfortable boundaries, confirming to Coughlin that it had been a wise idea to create it. Acknowledging it as necessary and liking it were two completely separate things, however.

"Bind the territory to Hell and he's all yours. He should be sufficiently weak at this point that he'll be unable to ever escape. See that he stays that way."

The creature licked its cracked lips with its terrible forked tongue, a hint of unnecessary glee in its eyes. Coughlin turned and took one last look at the pitiful soul of the boy.

"When God re-opens the gates of Eden and welcomes humanity back once more, I pray he sees fit to forgive you."

With that, the Priest left the soul to its judgment.

COUGHLIN RETURNED TO the Cathedral of Saint Giovanni and took a deep breath. The smell of the burning incense calmed his soul, though it did not fully remove the cries of the damned that echoed in his mind. This job had never been easy, and it seemed of late to continually grow harder.

"You're troubled, my brother?"

Giovanni's voice rung out unexpectedly, but so soft and soothing that Coughlin never experienced the need to jump at its appearance. "No more than usual, I'm afraid."

Giovanni nodded sagely, placing a firm, comforting hand on his shoulder. "It is a hard burden you have undertaken. But aren't the worthy ones always so?"

Coughlin nodded, moving to sit in the hard wooden pews. Their solid presence always brought a measure of comfort. "I know. It's just..." He thought of the cries of the boy, the vague memories of a righteousness in his terrible deeds coupled with the guilt and misery of their results. "Sometimes I wish there were other means."

The warm saint sat next to him, his voice offering a measure of calmness that Coughlin very much needed in moments like this. "It is not ours to question, though, is it? Unless, that is, you intend to become God rather than usher his return?"

Coughlin shook his head, somewhat chastised at the thought. "No. Of course not."

"I know this." Giovanni smiled warmly. "But sometimes I feel you need to hear it aloud, yourself. You are but a righteous tool of the Lord. If you trust in him, you may bend, but you will not break. If you trust, you will succeed, and yours shall usher in an era of peace and glory such as has not been seen since the gates of Paradise were closed."

"Yes. Trust in the cause. This must work out."

"It will work, my Brother. Now, focus not on those who remorsed their sins too late. Focus on those whose souls you have freed. Think of those whom this fallen one wronged, and how they will rest eternally knowing that the transgressions against them received the punishment they deserved."

Giovanni was right, of course. Those whose terrible experiences he excised were now truly joyful in their afterlife. Something that they had not been able to achieve since their tragic deaths occurred. He would try to focus on their joy, rather than the suffering of the damned. It was a hard thing to do, given that he did not always have a link to the lighter parts of their souls that remained. So instead he focused on the memories he had of them, the first sight of their burdens being lifted from them and the joy returning to their faces.

Those memories often felt small compared to the horrors he still sensed at the edge of his own being, but it would have to be enough. It would be enough. Wouldn't it?

Chapter 5

Jack waited as the reunion among his trio settled down. Jacob stood uncharacteristically willing to accept the bear hug from Huang. Heather turned back to him with a smile.

"Holy crap balls, Jack. I thought you said you couldn't bring him back."

"Aye." Jack nodded, taking his usual seat in the corner of the mental bungalow that once again served as their meeting room. "And I wasn't completely lying about that."

"What the hell do you mean? He's right there." She turned back and raised an eyebrow at Jacob. "You are right there, right?"

Jacob pulled himself away from Huang. "Yeah. Well, sorta. It's a strange story, Red."

Heather spun and took a seat on the bed, looking back at Jack. "Well, I do love a good story." Jack could tell by her eyes that she remained both curious and suspicious of what that story might entail.

He had debated how much to tell them. There was always the chance that a member of the counsel might betray him and forcefully take their memories. If that happened, it could greatly compromise his plans if they knew much.

But he had promised to always be honest with them when this started. He didn't wish to change that now. It was already getting difficult to remember what it had been like to just be "Jack", the trainer and de facto leader of the Order of the Shield. He had fought his entire death to keep anyone from getting the level of power he now possessed, under the belief that it would corrupt them and endanger others. He could not completely trust that his own viewpoint would not become compromised. The best way to minimize that risk would be to stick as closely as possible to the plans he made before taking on the Helm of Hades.

That meant keeping his team informed, no matter the risk.

"Aye lass. Well, for starters I figured out what they did to poor Domi. He was a construct created from memories and tied to the memory of me. Anyone who had memories of me could see him. Since the council had all taken in Domi's original memories, they could see him just as well as we could. No one else in this realm had that ability."

"That's interesting, Jack, but how's it relevant?" Jack could tell by the look in Heather's eyes that she suspected, but wanted him to actually say it.

Huang beat him to it. "Jacob is a construct. Like Dominique."

Heather looked back and forth between Jack and Jacob, before setting her narrowed eyes on Jack. "Is that true?"

Jack nodded.

Heather turned back to Jacob. "And you're okay with this?"

"Hell, Red, I'm still not sure I even believe it. But yeah. It's crazy, but for now I'll deal with it."

Heather nodded. Even actively trying not to read his links to them, Jack could still feel her discomfort about her friend's fate pushing through. "So how's this help us, Jack?"

"We need to start a war. The quicker the better. It's the only chance we have of getting out of here."

"Okay. And?" Jack wasn't certain if it was a testament to their trust in him or just lack of concern with details that neither Heather nor Huang felt the need to ask "why".

"And, lass. You did some marketing when you were alive. How would you have sold a war?"

Heather's smile scared him more than a little. "It's been done a thousand times. Why mess with the formula? Dehumanize your enemy, stoke fear of them coming for something you believe is yours, and then introduce a threat or attack to set the whole thing on fire."

"Aye." Jack nodded. "We have our enemy. There's a fair bit of nervousness around them since the centuries long war they fought before. Our job's to stoke this fear back up."

"And I trust you've considered the consequences of being successful at that?"

"Aye, Lass. From every angle. It's better than the alternatives, trust me."

"Fine." Heather nodded. "But what's this got to do with Jacob not getting his full soul back?"

"He's going to be our spy. I've tied his memory to that of my former student Thomas. I never told Domi about bringing him on, so no one out there should be able to see him."

"I did not know him either." Huang added in one of his rare verbal interjections.

"No, lad. You didn't. That means that outside of this room, neither of you will be able to see him either."

"A ghost among ghosts, eh?" Heather asked snidely as she turned back to Jacob. "You better not spy on me in the bathroom."

"You're dead, Red. Why the hell would you be in the bathroom?"

The red head shrugged. "I don't know. But if I do, you better not be there."

Jacob laughed, perhaps for the first time since Jack had brought him back from oblivion. "Deal. I think I can manage that.'

Jack felt Huang pondering a question. He knew that in most circumstances the big man would assume Jack had the answer, but he'd experienced enough of Huang's keen observation skills to know all of them should at least be shared. So he gave him a mental push to go ahead and voice his concern.

"Won't the council wonder at you not bringing Jacob back?" The big man looked somewhat surprised at his own voice.

'Good question lad, " It was, and Jack hoped to reinforce the kid into speaking up more often. "Normally yes, but I've been playing around a wee bit with my powers. I'm pretty sure that I have been able to rewrite the history of our time here slightly so that everyone else believes that final test they gave me with Domi actually ended with Jacob's death. It won't hold up too well to scrutiny, but these bastards should have no reason to think about it too hard if we are careful."

"Fair enough." Heather nodded. "I'm game with whatever you need. I just ask two things."

"What's that, Lass?"

"You bring all of us in here periodically to catch up, and you agree that when all of this is done, you'll make Jacob a real boy again."

Jack nodded with a smile. "I'll do my best with both."

"All I can ask from you. Now, what do you need us to do."

Jack had been dreading that question. "Yes. About that..."

Chapter 6

"Come with me".

Buster's voice held an air of authority and command, such that Thomas didn't think to question or even read the dog's thoughts for their destination. He merely did as the dog instructed and began to follow. It took a moment for his curiosity to catch up with him.

"Where are we going?"

The German shepherd didn't answer, instead nuzzling its head underneath Thomas's hand. When a firm enough connection formed, the dog shifted, and Thomas's world blurred.

When the world re-solidified, Thomas quickly realized that they were back in the Prime, but beyond that he could not determine where they were. A single object, a crib, suddenly brought it all into focus.

"Why did you bring me here?"

"It has been three months since your child left the hospital. You have not seen her since."

Thomas backed away, though he had a hard time placing his nervousness. "We've been busy."

"No." Buster stated in his usual 'matter-of-fact' tone. "You are scared."

Thomas started to rebuke him, explain all the reasons why that wasn't the case, but he stopped. The dog had watched over him from the time he had occupied his own crib. Even without their mutual link, Thomas could hide next to nothing from him. Even, he realized, things he had grown adept at hiding from himself.

"I had a vision back when we saw that seer, Stella." He hadn't considered it to be a big deal before, but now, as he thought about it, he realized how much it had affected him. "I didn't know what to make of it then, but I'm afraid I might now."

The dog nodded. "What do you think you saw?"

Thomas shuddered as he recalled the site. "I stood back at the Glacier of Gods and Monsters. Except I wasn't really me." New details fell into place as he thought back to the vision. " I think I was a massive version of Senebkay. And there were three more massive figures there. One was Brother Coughlin, the second Jack, and the third looked like Cleopatra for some reason. I don't know, but it seemed like we were all four about to fight each other. Then the Glacier began collapsing and..."

Thomas looked over at the crib and choked up slightly. "... and I saw people below us begin dying. And I didn't care. She was there, as was her mother. I saw them scream. I saw them die in agony. I didn't care. They're the two most important people to me in all of creation, Buster, and I watched in apathy as they ceased to be in the River. "

Buster took in this revelation, quiet for a moment, before finally replying, "The Great Spirit once told me that visions were glimpses in the moonlight. They offered some truth, but cannot be trusted to look the same under the light of day."

"How much truth? Will I fight Jack and the others? Will I be forced to become Senebkay to have a chance of winning? Will that little girl pay the price for all of this? How much of that will come to be?"

Buster shook his furry head. "I do not know, Thomas."

Thomas pushed himself forward, half hoping that the child would not be there, that she would be down the hall with her mother in the room they had shared when they were alive.

As he looked over the edge of the crib, he saw her. His baby. The last living piece of him drawing breath in the world. She was beautiful and perfect and she absolved all fear and anxiety he had at being near her.

She also increased the anxiety he had that she may come to harm because of his actions.

"I'm doing this for her, Buster." He whispered the words; afraid of waking her despite knowing she would never know his voice. "I'll sacrifice everything about myself if it means keeping her safe. But now I've got this nagging fear... what if the very thing I'm doing is what will put her in danger?"

"This is not what I know, Thomas. I have never experienced this choice you have. But I know someone who did. You were asked to free the Great Spirit from his fate. If you can do this, he may be able to answer your questions before departing."

Thomas nodded. He had not thought of the old Medicine Man in some time. He could not begin to guess what it would take to fulfill the Native American's wish for him, but there was no doubt that Falling Dusk was the best chance he had at getting answers. Few would have experience with what he was going through, and the only other soul he knew for certain that did was unlikely to provide him any assistance he could trust.

"Okay then. How do we find the Great Spirit?"

Buster sat oddly quiet for a moment. "I do not know for certain. He has not spoken to me since our connection was... severed. I will return to where I last heard his voice, and I will see what I can find. "

"Great. Let's go."

"No, Thomas." The dog shook his head again. "It is better that I do this alone. There are dangers to you that I am unlikely to stir. You will know if your help is needed. Spend this time with your daughter. You will not have many of these moments. Trust me. I was once a father too."

Thomas raised his eyebrow. "How did I not know this?"

The dog looked away. "Much time has passed. I chose to be a warrior. I made the choices I felt needed to be made to protect my family's safety. Just as you now do."

Thomas reached down and scratched the large dog behind his ear. "Thanks buddy."

With that the dog vanished.

Thomas turned back to the crib, looking at the beautiful little creature laying within. It surprised him to see her awake this time, and staring up in his direction.

"You are so amazing, you know that?" He could have sworn that she tilted her head slightly in his direction. "You know, if I didn't know better I would think you could hear me."

Charlotte giggled, and whether or not it truly was meant for him, Thomas's heart melted all over again.

Chapter 7

"This makes no sense." Mikon mumbled, playing with the reddish trim on his robe. Jack now knew that the once great politician often did that when nervous. "We have been happy with our truce for generations. Why would Set choose to break it now?"

Jack had assembled the council at Crisa's recommendation. Or at least, she felt it was her recommendation. He had learned enough about her from his connections to know that she was at her best when following she her own ideas. So far, the council meeting had not disappointed him. Each sat at a round table in the primary throne room. Though Jack's sat closest to the throne itself, as befitting his position as the current Hades, the circular table made it clear that there was meant to be no true leader of the council.

The group still impressed Jack, despite himself. The history locked in their collective minds stunned him every time he thought about it. Crisa had run a ranch in Greece some three thousand years prior. Mikon had been one of the early Greek orators and statesmen. The mighty warrior Argos was also Greek, having lived and ultimately died as a hoplite.

The impressive Teleklos appeared as a well-built man in his fifties. The cloth draped over his left shoulder looked regal, befitting his title prior to his death of King of the Spartans. Next to him sat the Persian King, Darius, whose many jewels made for an interesting difference from the Spartan king.

The beautiful and fiery Golnar sat next to him. In life she had been the high priestess of a tribe that wondered the Middle East through lands that had long since disappeared from maps.

An olive-skinned woman named Katina, with unnaturally blue eyes, rounded out the council. A peasant of Persia in life, she had long ago made herself feel at home among royalty in death.

These were the souls Jack must work with to achieve his goals. These were the people he would need to manipulate if he had a chance to go home. They played their secrets extremely close to the vest despite their connection to him. But the thousands of years that separated their lives did not seem to change much of what it meant to be human. Jack found their reactions to be remarkably predicable.

"She's testing our boundaries!" The mighty Argos shouted while he pounded his breastplate. "She's looking to see if our new ruler is weak! We should respond with a show of force that will settle all questions."

The former Spartan king, Teleklos, nodded in agreement. "Yes. It's been obvious that she has chaffed at this so-called 'truce' since the day we agreed to it. She will never be satisfied until she alone rules all. I say we take the fight to her."

Crisa shook her head wearily. "Have you forgotten the last war? Because I have not. It drained every one of us beyond measure, and we barely contained her fury then. Our numbers have dwindled, as has our will..."

"Speak for yourself." Argos spat.

"Fine." Crisa replied diplomatically. "As has my will, and no doubt some others. My point is that nothing has changed in our favor since the last war. What makes you certain that the results would be more positive this time around?"

"That is not entirely true." This came from the sultry voice of Golnar. "We have our new leader, and his warriors. I'm curious to hear what his take on this would be."

That caught Jack by surprise. He had expected old habits to die hard, and the council to focus on its long-standing members, almost to the point of ignoring him completely. It seemed he might not have a completely solid read on each of them after all.

Still, he had been giving the approach a lot of thought, so he wasn't completely caught off guard. "We must be careful. Set may very well be trying to goad us into action before we decipher her entire plan..."

"Bah." Argos hissed. Jack raised his hand to placate the hotheaded warrior.

"But, our warriors and kings have a point. We've lost a hand full of souls along the eastern board. There's a chance this isn't the first power she's taken from us, only that this is the first we've become aware of. If she continues and we do nothing, she may steal enough souls to tip the balance.

"Perhaps we should send an envoy." Whispered Katina. She had been the one to originally negotiate the current truce with Set. It was not surprising that she would seek to do the same now. Jack, in fact, had counted on it. "She suffered as much as us during the last war. Chafe or not, she can be reasoned with and if she knows her actions may lead to her destruction, perhaps she'll cease.

"Or perhaps she'll just take the envoy and laugh at us." Argos growled.

"I'll send my team." Jack intervened, to the surprise of many of council. "Heather and Huang. Look, it seems obvious we can't just sit on our bloody arses and do nothing. But starting a war without at least trying to avert it may get us all killed. Heather and Huang are tied directly to me, and I can draw the most power of any of us right now. That makes them safer than anyone else. They get into trouble, I yank them back. If I fail, we know for sure she's getting too powerful and we may have no choice but to make a final stand. If they can talk her into stopping though..."

Crisa nodded. "I do not like the potential here, but it seems the best course of action. I am in favor."

"It is the smart choice." Katina added.

Telekos nodded. "It is not wise to start a battle without first scouting one's enemy. I will agree."

Mikon added his assent, as did the typically quiet Darius. All eyes turned to Argos. There were more than enough votes to set the council's action, however Jack had noted their preference for unanimous consent.

"Fine." He growled. "Least it won't be anyone we'll miss. But if we don't prepare for the likelihood that this will lead us to war, then you're all fools."

Jack nodded. "I agree. Hope for the best, plan for the worst. I'll let my people know their mission. "

With that Jack teleported out before the council could erupt into debate again.

Chapter 8

"You do not belong here anymore, Brother."

Buster kept himself from jumping as the brave materialized next to him. He had expected that he might encounter resistance approaching the Great Spirit's cave, but he had not expected it to be this far out. He pushed down his urge to growl at the spirit that represented both a tribe he fought in life and a soul he had been linked to in death.

"I have business with the Great Spirit."

"No, you do not." The man slammed his spear down in the ground between them. "The Great Spirit is no more. Only the Great Bear remains, and he holds no desire to speak with the lesser spirit of another."

Buster shook his head, then stood up to two legs, transforming himself back into the Native Warrior of his first life. "I am only the spirit of another because the Great Spirit deemed it so. I do my duty as he requested. But now my duty demands that I speak with him, just as I have many times before."

Buster started to move past the brave, but the man sidestepped to remain in front of him. He did not make a move to attack, but his body language made it clear that he would not mind the chance.

"Move aside."

"If, as you say, you have moved on due to orders from the Great Spirit, then I would suggest you continue back to your new master, as ordered. The Great Bear rumbles at the edge of my mind even now, wild as he has been for centuries. He does not wish to see you. Were you to make it past me, he would greet you only with tooth and claw."

Much about the brave's comment struck Buster as impossible. "You say that the Bear has been wild for centuries. Yet he has instructed me not a Summer past."

The brave shook his head. "The Great Bear has not 'spoken' to anyone since the Final Battle."

Buster knew that comment to be ridiculous. He felt his normal calm begin to falter. "Do you doubt my words?"

"Tell me the last time you saw the Great Spirit, Brother?"

"I told you, he spoke to me as recently as..."

The brave raised his hands "Saw. With your own eyes. When did he last stand before you as I do now?"

Buster considered it. He had stood outside the Great One's cave many times over the past thirty years since he awakened. The Great Spirit's voice had always rung out clearly to him each of those times. But now that he thought about it, he could not remember actually seeing the Spirit since before the Final Battle.

The look on his face must have served as the answer that the Brave in front of him expected. "I thought as much. You still have the feel of the Great Spirit on you. I know what sacrifices you made. That is the only reason I give you this warning. "

Buster began to consider that maybe he had read the brave's intentions incorrectly. "What warning is that?"

"Few of us remain ourselves these days. One of the elders told us that the Great Spirit released a number of his spirits prior to the Great Battle, knowing what his price would be for victory. Your discussions with the Great Spirit were not last year. They were before the Final Battle. You only experienced them recently."

Buster considered this, along with the information Thomas had told him about his dream of the Great Spirit. It made a strange form of sense.

"The Great Spirit won the battle. But he did not escape it. He and those of us remaining were severed from our Spirit Realms."

Buster did not like the sound of that. He had encountered souls cut from the Spirit realm before. They became very dangerous and unstable. "How is it that you can talk to me about this?"

"I do not know." The brave shrugged honestly. "There are a small band of us who retain our selves. A medicine man among us believes that perhaps we too were part of the plans the Great One put into place. Maybe I am only here to stop you from moving forward on this day."

The brave reached over and grabbed his spear. "What I do know is that if you proceed, your new connection will make you a target for those who know only rage. If you somehow survive them... The Great Bear is not the Great Spirit. The Great Spirit died in the taking of the God Monk. Only his rage and will to survive remain. You will not find what you seek in him."

It was not what he had hoped to find, but it explained what the Great Spirit might have wanted with Thomas Salazar. "What did they call you when you last walked among men?"

"Falling Sparrow."

"Thank you, Falling Sparrow." Without waiting for a reply, Buster returned to his canine form and dashed back onto the Great Path.

Had he glanced behind him, he might have caught the morphing of the young brave's features into that of a much older, more familiar figure. "Farewell, Running Wolf. May you end that which I started."

Chapter 9

Thomas returned to Leo's plateau with a rejuvenated sense of purpose. Spending time with his daughter had been magical. He still couldn't explain how it might be the case, but he'd become convinced that she could actually hear and see him.

Perhaps it was merely wishful thinking; perhaps just that babies were so new to the Prime that they still retained some small connection to the River. Whatever the reason, it made his heart soar to think about the giggle coming from her tiny lips.

He would have likely stayed there much longer, had the sense of urgency in Leo's tugs not gotten more and more emphatic.

The small Italian could barely contain himself when Thomas finally stepped out.

"Thomas! You came back! Good, there is still time!"

Thomas stopped himself from asking what there was 'still time' for when he noticed someone new standing on the platform. A short man, just a bit on the squat side, with an olive complexion and a dark pencil thin mustache looked on from where Leo had been standing. He wore a close fitting black pinstriped suit with a white necktie and a black fedora.

He looked like the walking definition of sleazy. Thomas didn't trust him, and barely resisted ransacking Leo's memories to determine how much of a threat the man might be.

If the man noticed Thomas's reaction, he didn't let it show. He swaggered over, extending a greasy looking palm. "Eh, you must be the new big cheese. Shame to hear bout Jack. Stand up kinda guy. "

Thomas took the extended hand, trying to suppress his feeling of disdain. "Err... yeah. We still feel his loss."

"Dan Capone. I'm what you might calls an 'Acquirer'. A finder of talent if you wills. Ole Leo here, he tells me you needs a soul who can read the signs.

One with which you can speed talk into helping you. I think you may be in luck. One's coming on the market soon."

Thomas could not entirely figure out where this conversation was going, nor did he feel certain that he liked its direction. Before he could ask anything though, Leo grabbed his arm. "Dan, if you excuse me. I must be filling in Thomas on things."

"Meh." The gangster wannabe shrugged. "No skin off my nose. I'll just be watching your fishes then."

He turned at that and wandered back to the pond. Leo led Thomas back a ways. "My apologies, Thomas. I had hoped to pull you back before his arrival. But as usual he is early, and unfortunately you were late."

"So you've worked with this guy before?"

Leo nodded. "We've used him in the past. He comes to us now and then when he knows of someone dying that he thinks we might want to recruit. I see the look in your eye, Thomas. I know it because Jack held the same look. I'll tell you what I used to remind him: Dan's not very nice; he is shady and he is often obnoxious to be around. But at his job, Thomas, there are few better. "

"And his job is finding souls?"

"Specific souls, yes." Leo nodded. "He's got a gift for both reading souls while they're in the body, and knowing when their time is near an end."

"And he does this out of the goodness of his heart?"

Leo shook his head. "Death, Thomas, it is like life. When people do something, something is in it for them."

Thomas nodded. "I thought as much. What do we pay for these services?"

Leo shrugged. "We accept that he is what he is. We may also occasionally help him avoid people who dislike him."

Thomas nodded. "Many of those, are there?"

Leo nodded, but it was Senebkay, popping back in from seemingly out of nowhere, that answered.

"Of course there is. He kills people."

"He what?" Thomas turned back to his other self, forgetting for a moment that Leo could not hear that part of the conversation.

"He kills people. Probably killed us." Senebkay said with a twisted smile. "I know his type. Used a few of them myself back in my time as Ra. "

Thomas suddenly felt even more uncomfortable with this "acquirer" than he had been. "What exactly do you mean he killed us?"

"Your other half," Leo said looking in the general direction of Senebkay. "I take it he is here?"

Thomas nodded. "Yes. He says he knew souls like Dan over there, and that they can somehow kill people. Is that right?"

Leo seemed reluctant to answer. "The truth, it is a bit more complex than that. He can... speed up what is already happening."

"He kills people." Senebkay added flatly.

"So he can kill people." Thomas reiterated to Leo. He never really knew how much of Senebkay's view to take as fact.

Leo shrugged. "He can see when people are near death, Thomas. This process, he can speed up for them. But only them."

'How much can he speed this up?"

"A day maybe. Two at the most, as near as I can tell."

"I told you." Senebkay smiled. "Now ask about us."

"Did he kill me?" Thomas asked, raising his eyebrow.

Leo shifted uncomfortably. "With certainty, Thomas, I do not know."

Thomas felt his face begin to flush with anger, as if he still had blood to boil. "But you think he did, don't you?"

"Thomas, calm down, please. Let me tell you more."

Thomas fought to keep himself calm. It was more difficult than it should be. He looked over towards this Dan Capone. The man stood staring into the pond while smoking a cigarette, completely oblivious to the conversation going on about him. Before he could Thomas could decide whether to attack him or not, Senebkay stayed his hand.

"Do calm down as the man says, Thomas." The pharaoh sounded almost bored. "It won't do to attack such a useful soul just yet. Business is business, and we can use him. Then we can kill him."

"Fine. Tell me your story, Leo." He reframed once again from just taking the information from the Italian's memories.

"Our ranks, they were thinning. You know this. Capone, he told us you would be dying soon, and that you had potential to fit in with us. Jack followed up and agreed. When you died, Jack followed you over to be there."

"Did he kill me?"

"It is possible, Thomas. But you were to die anyway. And it may have been far worse had he not."

Thomas could barely control himself. "WORSE? My fiancée was going to tell me she was pregnant THAT NIGHT! We could have celebrated. Had one last memory together. HOW COULD IT HAVE BEEN WORSE?"

"She could have died too, Thomas." Leo said with a sigh. "Jack, he felt as you did. He was reluctant to use Dan early on, even if we had used him before. So he insisted on learning more."

Leo tried to be as soothing as he could through the link, though Thomas suspected the man had no idea that he was doing so. "This gift, Thomas, Jack watched it. He reported back what he found, which matched up with others I have seen study it.

Capone knows who will certainly die. He can subtly affect them to speed it up. But he does not know who might die. He would point out when this was going to happen to Jack, and Jack would watch. In all cases, the target would die. In some cases the target died alone. In others it they died in ways that affected many others. One, he drove a bus, and died at the wheel. Another, he worked in demolitions. The explosives that he mishandled," Leo shrugged, "they took out more than just him."

Leo placed a comforting hand on Thomas's shoulder. "You may have died driving your wife around, and brought her with you. Or you may have died in bed next to her, where she would have had to find you. There are many worse fates, Thomas, and we do not know until it is too late what yours would be. If you were taken early, and I say again that this is an if, it might have been far for the better."

Thomas tried to take in Leo's words, to decide what should really feel. On the one hand, he continued to be furious at the prospect that he might have missed even a few more hours with Shari. On the other hand, he felt a creeping horror of how he would have dealt with being the one who killed Shari and their newly conceived child. How horrible would that have been?

"For what it's worth." Senebkay added nonchalantly, "he's likely telling the truth. I've used many of his kind before, and what Leo describes is accurate. That doesn't mean we shouldn't send him back into the River on principle."

"Fine." Thomas stated, more petulantly than he intended. "I trust you and Jack did your research on this guy. We'll use him."

Leo smiled, a sense of relief flooding through their shared link. "A good decision for you to make, Thomas. Let us discuss our new prospect."

Chapter 10

"Did you see the legs on that bird? What I wouldn't do to still have some blood flow, know what I mean? Of course you do. We're almost there, it's just... whoa, hey baby...."

Thomas tried his best to tune Dan Capone out. The man had entered the Prime some miles ago, and had been moving at a slow pace ever since. When he wasn't gawking at and making lewd comments towards every female they walked past he was bragging about himself. Capone painted himself as a high level member of a crime family back in the 20's. His tales strained belief, and moved all over the map, leading Thomas to surmise that at best he'd probably been a two bit hoodlum, and most of the stories being told were likely just that, stories.

"Glad to see you living up to your potential, kiddo. I tolds Jack, I said 'this kid's got potential.' And look at you. Leading the whole shebang now. Have I got an eye or what? Of course I do, and you'll see with your knew recruit. I sense him right up here. He's... there."

Thomas looked ahead at a crowded sidewalk full of people. "Which one am I supposed to be looking at?"

"I would say the negro kid with the poor sense of fashion, but that doesn't narrow it down, am I right?" Dan laughed at his own joke. Thomas grimaced. "But seriously, hang on, I'll make him stand out for ya's."

Capone looked around then pointed at a kid playing basketball coming towards them. Dan walked up next to him, and with a swipe that seemed like it was easier than Thomas suspected it was, Capone somehow managed to send the ball spinning out into traffic. "Go get it kid."

As if the child could actually hear him, the kid dashed into the road in a frantic attempt to wrangle his wayward ball. Thomas was so astounded that Capone had managed to have an affect on something in the real world that he almost missed the oncoming bus barreling a bit too quickly down the road towards the boy.

"And queue the heroics!"

Again, as if responding to Capone's statement, a black man in his late twenties or early thirties dashed out of the crowd that Capone had pointed to a few minutes earlier. He wore tight, distressed jeans and a form fitted muscle shirt. The man moved with enough grace to show that he was used to moving. He gave the kid a shove at the last minute, but Thomas could only watch in horror as he realized that there was no way for the man to save himself.

Two long seconds, some squealing breaks, a loud horn and a number of screams later the bus came to a stop, but the man had ceased to move. Thomas's horror was interrupted by Capone's scream of success.

"And he even managed to keep the kid alive! I am GOOD! Alright kid, keep your nose clean. Let me know if you're looking for anybody else."

Thomas turned away from the graphic scene in front of him, unable to disguise the look of bewildered horror in his eyes. "What?"

"The kid's sanctuary door will, of course, open right above him. If you hurry, you can probably be there before he really realizes that he's dead." Dan stopped talking for a moment as his eyes followed a young woman in a short skirt hurrying away from the scene. "Now if you'll excuse me, I think I'm going to go take in a show."

With that the creepy soul wondered off in the same direction as the young lady. Thomas shook his head, wondering again why Leo had felt the need to work with him. He hoped that the results, however tragically obtained, were worthwhile. He reminded himself of what Leo had told him, that this could only have played out if the kid they were trying to recruit was about to die soon anyway. At least he died a hero. Maybe some small conciliation could be earned from that.

Thomas put the two-bit gangster out of his mind and focused on the task at hand. He knew absolutely nothing about the recently deceased young man, but he trusted Leo's judgment enough to believe the man would be of help to them. Plus, he remembered how much it helped to have Jack there to greet him when he passed over. Maybe now he could return the favor to someone else.

He steeled himself for a moment, calming his mind. Then, attempting to see as little of the man's damaged body as possible, he walked through the crowd of gawkers and stepped into the newly shimmering portal.

Chapter 11

"Oh Lord Hades, Ruler of the Realm below and the land above, I beseech thee, end my suffering."

Jacob stood quietly in the corner of the small hut, watching the old man pound the ground rhythmically with his prayer.

"Oh Lord Hades, Last of the True Gods, I beseech thee, end my suffering."

The man looked to be in his late forties, and wore only a simple tunic that may have never been washed. He had been going on with this since Jacob arrived. He doubted the man could sense him, but it made him wonder just how long he had been carrying out this chant. His cousin, whom Jacob had collected earlier in the day, had made it clear that this man, Brodivus, had recently lost his only child to a cart accident. He had not taken it well. Jacob could only assume that had been the start of it.

Jacob knew that he would be the end of it.

Jack had charged him with collecting souls. He needed to quietly remove them from the pool, in an effort to frame the so-called god of Egypt for their disappearances. His work was not likely to get noticed at first. Like cutting just a few small hairs from a sleeping person, they would not feel the loss when it occurred, but they would certainly notice the results after awhile.

Jack had left it open as to how Jacob coducted his new job as the angel of death. The new Hades only cared that the work be done.

"Oh Lord Hades, just and fair lord, I beseech thee, take me back."

Jacob had felt uncomfortable killing the innocent, even if they were already dead. This mimicry of life came across like a form of what it imitated, and it felt completely wrong for him to take it, even on Jack 'Hades Almighty' himself's orders. But, he had quickly realized that the world was full of people like Brodivus. People who suffered for one reason or another and no longer wanted the existence they had received.

If Jacob had to take souls, then he might as well be an angel of mercy in his role of Death.

He held out his hand and materialized the infinitely black blade. The dark energy extended an inch above his hand, deadly to the touch but safe at that distance. It perfectly mimicked the blade that had been used to cut his own connection to Jack when he'd faced Argos. He'd known then that it was an unlikely fight for him to win then. He now realized it had been impossible odds. He had stood as much a chance of winning then as Brodivus stood of opposing him now.

None.

With a shake of the head, Jacob waited for one more round of pleas, and then gently sliced the silver cord coming from the man's back. Brodivus now became something almost unheard of in the realm. An Unclaimed.

While the older man had no way of knowing exactly what had been done to him, he could most certainly feel that something had suddenly changed. Like most of the others Jacob had collected, the man looked up, wild-eyed.

"Who... who's there?"

Jacob quickly reached down and established his own connection. An unclaimed running around would most certainly draw attention. Someone connected to him, would not. The man could have fought it. He wouldn't have stopped it, but he could have at least made the link unstable. He didn't of course. Jacob's link felt close enough to that of Hades for it to be natural, and the man welcomed it.

Truth be told, Jacob believed the man would have welcomed a link even from Set herself. Having spent his entire existence linked into a community, even being paired to his mortal enemy would have likely been preferable to being left alone.

Once the link formed completely, the man could do something else few in this realm could manage. He could see the other soul in the room with him.

"I am the Ferryman." Jacob had tried to tell people the truth early on, but he'd learned from the experience that things went far smoother when he merely played the part of their belief system. "I have come to fulfill your request."

"Hades be praised." Brodivus exhaled with an exhausted sigh. "Thank you, kind sir. Thank you."

"Take to your bed." Jacob replied as regally as he could manage. It felt wrong to lie to the man, but again he had found it far easier to play the part. "It would not do to have your neighbors find you in the floor."

"Thank you. Thank you, sir! Here!" The man hastily reached into a pouch at his waist and pulled two coins out in his grimy hands. "I have your payment, sir. That I may join my son!"

"Keep it." Jacob would not accept the coins even if they had had value to him. It was one thing to lie about who he was. It was another to be paid for his lie about the man's fate. "I will collect them when you reach the ferry."

Which would be never, but that was something the man did not need to know. In all likelihood, even had the man died naturally in this world, he would not have been reunited with his son. Jack had begun draining the underworld of its souls, boosting his power for the plans he had ahead. The council apparently found it a distasteful place, and so rarely paid more than passing attention to it. As soon as Brodivus's son passed beyond the care of the 'real' ferryman, Jack would likely have either recycled him back as a newborn or took the energy for himself.

The man dutifully laid himself down on his bed, and placed the two coins over his eyes. "I'm ready."

Jacob nodded his head, and solemnly placed his hand over the man. He quickly and painlessly ended Brodivus's life. He took all of that had truly made the man unique and pulled it through their shared link. He kept the strength, but channeled all of the negative emotions and memories into the blade. It glowed so brightly black for a moment that it darkened the room's candles before he hid its existence.

When he finished he looked down at the husk that had held the man. Neighbors would no doubt find him in the morning and bury him quickly. The council might notice the loss in power if they looked close enough, but it would be near impossible for them to determine where the loss occurred, much less follow up on how it happened.

They were unaccustomed to the unknown, and that would no doubt feed very easily into Jack's plans. It seemed even gods wanted easy answers, and having an enemy you wanted to believe the worst in always made for the quickest way to fill in the gaps.

Jacob had no issues at all lying to them. It was one of the few things that made his current role bearable. Their hubris had lead to all of the issues these people now experienced.

He only hoped that, when the time came, he could play the role of their angel of death as well.

For now, there was more business at hand. Jacob combed through the many memories of the late Brodivus. One stood quickly out to him. Brodivus had taken care of an aunt. The woman was wasting away as it was, and Brodivus had felt a tinge of guilt at not having checked in on her the last few days.

Jacob would check in on her, and if Brodivus's memories of her proved accurate, then the Ferryman would end another soul's suffering.

Chapter 12

The blaring club music and the quick shifting lights were a serious distraction to Thomas's search. Even with that, however, he was surprised he had not yet been successful.

"Is it possible we wound up in the wrong sanctuary?" Thomas asked to the air around him. He had grown accustomed to talking to himself, since he never really knew if Senebkay was listening or not. The Egyptian part of himself popped up at near random times, so Thomas typically assumed the being always roamed near by.

If he was currently, he'd not shown himself in a while. Thomas had been roaming about what he had assumed to be the mysterious black man's Sanctuary, but had not located anyone who looked like the man who had given his life.

A massive throng of people packed the nightclub inspired sanctuary. A few were generic and repeated, but most seemed unique in the club. The realism and level of detail impressed Thomas. The lights flashed in a variety of rapid-fire changes, so much so that he wondered if it would have induced seizures in someone back in the real world. The DJ blasted techno for the most part, but changed occasionally to hip-hop or random dance mixes.

Thomas had no doubt that this club must have been based on a place the black man had frequented often. There seemed no other way that a newly dead soul could create this much so soon after death.

"You look lost, sugar." The voice was female. Thomas looked over and saw a black woman tending the bar, staring at him. Not his targeted soul, but perhaps an important automaton that could point him in the right way?

"I'm looking for someone." Thomas called out over the music. He chided himself as he remembered Senebkay pointing out that the dead did not need to shout to communicate, even in loud areas, but it just felt natural. Plus, he didn't know with for certain just how that worked with automatons.

"Of course you are, baby. Everyone in here is." If she was an automaton, she was well programmed. Thomas revised his thought. Homunculus maybe?

He smiled, trying to seem as natural as he could so that he did not go outside the parameters of her programing. "I'm looking for someone specific. Black guy, around my height, maybe a bit taller. He would be around thirty or so, muscular, possibly wearing jeans and a tight shirt."

"My my." The woman giggled. "You are specific. Does this dream boy have a name?"

Thomas shrugged. "I'm sure he does, but I don't know it. I'm betting you probably do though. I have a some information for him, so it's very important I find him."

Before the woman could answer, Senebkay showed up next to the bar holding someone else's drink. "I thought I would let you know that we're about to have company. Very unwelcome company I suspect."

As if on queue, the door busted open, and four men on horseback charged into the club, trampling those guests that were not quick enough to get out of the way. They were dressed in what appeared to be southern Civil War era regalia. The leader had his head shaved, and bore a number of Swastikas on the exposed parts of his skin. It struck Thomas as strange to realize that people might carry a predudice against skin color into an afterlife with no actual skin.

The leader stopped and shot the closest speakers with a more modern looking pistol, then screamed out. "Marcus! Where are ya, boy? I found some friends who want to help welcome you to the other side!"

"Shit. That's impossible." The bartender cursed.

"You know these guys?" Thomas asked, forgetting for a moment the bartender likely wasn't a full soul.

"Marcus! Get yo ass out here!"

"Guys, no." The woman replied. "Guy, yes. The skinhead's Billy Roberts. We grew up together, before he went all Nazi war boy on us."

Thomas sized up the four. Despite their numbers and appearance, they didn't seem to have much clue as to what they were doing. They were making no attempt as far as he could see to lock down or take over the sanctuary. Instead they were relying on tactics that probably would have worked well for them in the real world. They were not so useful in the world of the dead.

'He doesn't seem to like this Marcus person."

"I sort of pushed him down a flight of stairs. To be fair, he was threatening me at the time, and I didn't mean to kill him, it just... "

"Marcus!" Billy screamed, then shot a handful of cowering dancers. "I will tear this place up to find you!"

Thomas realized with a shock whom he was talking to. "You're Marcus?"

The woman nodded her head tentatively. "You help me get rid of these guys, and I'll listen to what you have to say."

Thomas still felt more than a bit of smoldering anger towards Dan. While he couldn't do much about the sleazy gangster, these men provided a welcome outlet.

He gave in to Senebkay's influence and spun from the bar. "Gentlemen!" He cried out with just a tinge of sarcasm that felt more natural than it should. Senebkay's influence seemed to be growing on him. "Marcus appears to be unavailable. Care if I take a message?"

The men pulled their horses up within a few feet of him and laughed together when looking down at him. "Hey Mexican. Who are you, one of Marcus's little boyfriends?"

"Just a concerned patron having a drink. This is your one and only chance. Leave and never come back and we'll call this even."

Billy raised his gun, a mere six feet from Thomas's head. "Listen here, you little wetback. You tell Marcus to get his little butt out here pronto or we will vaporize you." He cracked a near maniacal smile. "I can tell you from experience, even the dead can die."

Thomas couldn't imagine how scared he would have been in anything close to this situation when he had been alive. But he didn't live anymore. Nor did he feel the least bit concerned.

Thomas considered misting the entire area, turning the men into club dancers. That, however, might have put them closer to equal footing. Instead he did something he doubted any of them expected. He let loose a fireball that exploded in the middle of the horses, sending soldier and horsemeat scattering.

Now that he knew the real soul in this club, he had little concern with collateral damage. Marcus could always rebuild everything herself later.

"Wrong response." He smiled. The men picked themselves up, slowly from the floor, watching him. Clearly they had not expected that. One of them raised his pistol and fired it four times at Thomas. Thomas held his hand up and stopped the bullets as they left the gun. That would have been much more difficult had he been fighting someone with control of the sanctuary, but these buffoons were merely making a contest of wills, and with his resources to draw from, they had no chance in that area.

Thomas considered sending all four men back to the River. They probably deserved it, and he could feel Senebkay pushing him to. That last part more than anything else forced him to hold back.

"I lied. I'll give you one last chance. Leave now and I'll let you keep your existence. I'll be keeping tabs on you though. You invade one more sanctuary and..." Thomas held up his hand, creating another ball of fire in it, "next time I will end you. All of you."

If looks could kill the dead, the glare Billy gave him would have put him back in the River for certain. However, the man just stood up and dusted himself off. "Come on, boys."

All four glared as they left the Sanctuary by the bar's front door. Thomas let the ball of fire dissipate, then turned back to the female bartender who claimed to be 'Marcus'.

As he did, the world shifted, as much of a complete 180 degrees as it could. Instead of the now damaged dance club, Thomas found himself in a small but brightly lit church. The man he had witnessed give his life to save a little kid sat in the pew closest to him.

"You know," he started with a hint of sadness. "This is the only place where I never could bring myself to be Shantae. My mom would always try and shame me with 'God's watching you, you know!' but for the most part I didn't care. Except here. I guess because this was like His house, you know? I always felt the need to be Marcus here."

Thomas sat down next to the man and looked around. The room looked beautiful and filled him with a profound sense of calm and peace. Again, the detail told him that Marcus must have spent a lot of time here as well. "It's nice to meet you."

"I'm dead, aren't I?"

The statement came out very matter of fact. Thomas couldn't help but reply in the same way. "Yes. I'm afraid so."

"Not what I expected."

Thomas chuckled to himself. "No. It rarely is."

Marcus turned and looked Thomas over very carefully. "You don't look like St. Peter. Though that fight was impressive."

"Thanks." Thomas smiled. "But that's just practice, really. And no, as my mentor once said to me when I sat in your position 'I'm not a relative, nor am I an angel, crow, Valkerie, demon, or any other guide religion and folklore have come up with. I am exactly what you are. A projection of my last life."

"Just another lost soul then?"

Thomas nodded. "Yeah. Just another lost soul."

"Man." Marcus muttered. "This is one fucked up afterworld."

Thomas shrugged. "It has its advantages. You can see at least some of the people who passed before you." Thomas thought back to their entirely too recent encounter. "Though I suppose in your case that's not always going to be a good thing."

Marcus smiled. "Billy's a special case. Always has been, I suppose. But there is a guy I would like to find. My first boyfriend. He died close to ten years ago. Be nice to see him again."

Thomas nodded. "Well, I can try to help you with that. But I've got an offer for you first. It's dangerous, but if you're willing to listen, I think we can help each other out a lot."

Marcus looked up at the giant cross that dominated the front of the room. "Well, you did deal with Billy for me. It seems rude for me to not at least hear you out."

Thomas nodded. "Thanks. This could take a while to explain."

Marcus shrugged. "Apparently, I'm dead. So what do I care?"

Thomas smiled. "That's true. Okay then. Let me start."

Thomas attempted to fill Marcus in on the entire situation. He told him about Brother Coughlin and his war, Thomas's own training, the loss of Jack, and everything that had happened since. He tried to leave no details out. If Marcus was going to risk his soul with them, Thomas did not want there to be any false pretenses. Marcus, to his credit, remained a great listener. He asked occasional questions to clarify, but otherwise stayed silent and attentive.

Thomas did decide to leave out the part about watching Dan orchestrate his death. He understood why Jack would have not told him when they first met. He did not think he would have reacted well, nor did he trust Marcus to easily accept it either. But aside from that point he attempted to be as thorough as possible.

When he finished, he sat back in silence, giving Marcus an attempt to digest the information he had been given. "So... you think I have some skillz that you're lacking?"

Thomas nodded.

"And if I join you, I'll have to... join my soul to you? Like these other dudes have?"

Thomas nodded again. "It's the only way I know for sure we can keep you safe. I promise to respect your privacy as much as I can though."

"And if I say no?"

Thomas shrugged. "Then I leave. With any luck, Coughlin's not paying attention to us right now, so in all likelihood you would be left to enjoy your afterlife."

"Least till this Coughlin dude jacks it all up."

"If we fail." Thomas nodded. "Then yes. That's worst case scenario."

Marcus visibly weighed the pros and cons in his mind. Finally, after a few minutes of silence, he turned back to Thomas. "What the hell. I'm dead, right? I've got one condition though."

"What's that?" Thomas knew there was little he wouldn't do if he could to lock Marcus's assistance in.

"You teach me that fireball shit. That thing is OFF THE HOOK, man."

Thomas laughed, the first time he had genuinely done that in recent memory. "I'll do what I can."

"Yo, I can't ask for more than that." Marcus stood and extended a hand. "Let's do this thing."

Chapter 13

Heather stared out at the approaching landscape. "Holy crap balls. Look at that."

The sailors manning her vessel seemed entirely unimpressed by the impossibly large pyramid dominated the horizon, looking much like the mountains on the Greek side of the River.

"You guys have no appreciation for how awesome you have it here."

This entire adventure had been one astonishing site after another. Heather dreaded the idea that they couldn't return to the other side of the Glacier, but she had to admit that if the path were available, she wouldn't have chosen to take it just yet.

She had seen many absolutely phenomenal sanctuaries since her death, but the world on this side of the Glacier had been on a scale far and above anything she'd ever even suspected existed. The magnitude of size, the detail, the weird freaky costumes.... all of it added up to a spectacular site to behold.

"And we're sailing ON THE RIVER! How cool is that?" She thought, looking back at the uniquely colored roiling gaseous type substance that dominated three of the four directions.

Now that she knew what to look for, she could catch glimpses of the seams holding all of the different sanctuaries together. They were well worn, barely noticeable, but they were there.

She felt confident that with time, and a lack of interference, she could probably pull them all back apart. The lack of interference part, however, felt unlikely to happen. These self-proclaimed "gods" that stuck everything together would probably freak if she started pulling them apart again.

While making them freak sounded like a good thing for Jack's plans, he wanted them focused on each other, and not the team. Knowing she had the power to dismantle their stellar piece of art here piece by piece might bring far more attention from both sides than she wanted.

The thought of the sides brought Heather crashing back to her current mission. Jack had been very clear in the risks, and the safety precautions he had taken.

It was sweet of him to be so concerned, but she'd accepted the risks that came with this job long ago. As she liked to remind him, "We're already dead. There's no way we're getting out of here alive. "

It honestly surprised her that she'd made it through this long. And if you're going to lose your afterlife, losing it by pissing off an ancient Egyptian goddess had to count as one of the more interesting ways to go. Hopefully someone would survive from their retinue and make a good story out of it.

"How much longer?" She called out over her shoulder.

"We should be seeing land soon, Mistress Heather." A boy replied to her as he stretched out a length of rope for something. She felt a bit bad that she didn't remember any of the people's names on the boat. She'd been introduced to them yesterday when she boarded, but she was horrible with names in the best of cases. All of these people had bizarre ancient sounding names. There was no way she was going to be able to remember any of those. Luckily it didn't seem to matter. She could just call out questions in general and get a response from someone without any attempt at actually addressing any of the fifteen or so sailors by name.

"Thanks. What's it like?"

"Hot, usually." He replied, stopping his work to address her questions. She couldn't be certain if he welcomed the interruption or just felt he should be polite due to her known connection with his god and the council. "But not too busy. The Egyptians docks aren't really a center for commerce like ours."

Heather nodded and looked back over the slowly growing pyramid in the distance. She wished she had one of her companions to share the view with. Missions used to always be group events. More frequently in recent years they had been reduced to just pairs, but she did not remember ever doing something remotely this dangerous on her own before. Jack fanatically insisted everyone watch each other's back.

Of course, that had been before he had become a god. She supposed such things likely came with a shift in perspective. Not to mention the dramatic reduction in numbers their team had suffered. With Leo, Charlotte and their recruits stuck on the other side, and apparently all of their wayward companions here broken down and recycled, more than one person per mission became a luxury that Jack probably couldn't afford.

"Lady Heather." This came from one of the ship's few women, who called out to her as she rounded a corner. "We may have a problem." The woman walked up and handed her a fairly basic looking spy glass. Heather took it with a smile and a nod of gratitude.

She stopped herself from improving it dramatically. Now that she drew energy directly from Jack, and Jack drew from all of the souls he had access to, she once again had freedom to expend more without having to replace it. But Jack had asked her to limit such displays, since it apparently made the locals nervous.

Oh sure, they were fine with the idea that gods walked among them, but the idea that a soul could create something out of nothing had to be sorcery, and that had become as believable as it would have been in more superstitious areas of the Prime.

"What am I looking for?"

"There, Lady. On the shore ahead."

Heather followed the sailor's finger and searched the horizon with her spyglass. It didn't take long to spot the source of the woman's distress.. "So I'm assuming a hundred or so armed soldiers on the docks is not your usual greeting party?"

"No. It is very odd. A handful is customary. A phalanx's worth not unheard of. But I've never seen numbers like that."

Heather reviewed the horizon. She immediately saw a lot of soldiers, all standing with their oddly bent swords at the ready. She hadn't really known what to expect, so she decided this made as proper of a response as any. If they were like the Greek soldiers she'd faced with her team after first arriving in this realm all that time ago then it probably wouldn't be an issue. She had little doubt that she could take on a thousand of those and come out little worse for the ware. If they were more substantial.... Well, today was as good of a day to be recycled as any.

"How much longer till we arrive?"

"Twenty minutes if the wind holds. And it will, unless Set decides otherwise."

Heather closed the spyglass and handed it back. "It'll hold. You don't setup a welcome wagon like that and then stop your guests from arriving."

As she predicted, the wind held. "Thank Jack for small favors" she giggled. While the man might take her to task for joking about his god status, humor helped to lighten her mood. Waiting had never been one of Heather's strong points, and the steady rocking of the boat along with the view of her destination made juggling and other time killers more difficult to manage. In the end, she settled on studying the surroundings more, taking in all that she could.

She had never been to Egypt before. She felt reasonably certain that the real pyramids were not mountain size, but aside from that the rendition that lay spread out before her matched up with what she imagined the real Nile valley looked like. The River seemed to lap against the shore the way the the great river no doubt did in the real world, moving into a world where vibrant splashes of color broke up the otherwise uniformly brown landscape.

The shore approached faster than it probably would have in real life. For a boat with no visible means of power, her vessel made incredible speed. It didn't take long for the army of the shore to start coming into focus.

Not surprisingly, they had not moved at all. For all of the lifelike qualities this realm had, some weird small things remained missing. That necessary twitches of muscle movements, the need to shift your weight, nobody here seemed to have that. Probably something that other sanctuaries missed as well, now that she thought about it, but here, with the hyper real focus on things being so much more like the Prime, it became noticeable.

"We'll be at the docks in just a few minutes, Lady Heather."

Lady. She really could grow used to that. If only these folks knew. "Good deal. Drop the plank when we get there, but don't get off. I'll lead the way. If there's trouble, you may wish to attempt to leave."

"We are in Egypt, Lady Heather. If there is trouble, it is because Set wills it. If Set wills it, we will not be allowed to leave."

They probably had a point, but she still suggested they try it. It felt weird, they really weren't full souls, at least not in the way she was used to. But she still became kind of fond of them, despite their short time together.

Of course, if the boss had his way, they probably would all cease to be anyway. Recycled to the River and reborn anew. So she supposed there really was no helping their fate.

The final few minutes of travel stretched out like an eternity. Heather could barely contain all of the nervous energy she had as she wanted something, anything to happen. But nothing did. The wait stretched out to an excruciating length.

Finally, when she felt she could not handle the passage of time any more, the ship pulled into dock and the sailors of her ship quickly threw the boarding plank into place.

Heather almost leapt over the side before they finished, then danced down to the bottom to find herself facing off in front of the Egyptian military contingent blocking her path. She could tell by the lines of power that most of the soldiers here were actually connected through a handful of what must have been higher ranked officers. They would be the challenge, if fighting actually did break out.

In the end, she decided to push her luck and find out how quickly things were set to escalate.

"So. Umm. Yeah. You dudes probably know who I am by now, so... I don't know, take me to your leader?"

One of the officers stepped forward without a word. He raised his khopesh and nodded to her. She understood the motion well enough.

"So. A fight then, eh?" She drew her sabers with a smile. "And you're going to be kind enough to do it mook style? Hey, no arguments from me."

She barely finished the sentence before the man attacked. He moved fast, but no where near fast enough. Heather parried the blade and spun around, clocking him in the back of the head with the hilt of her sword. A quick glance confirmed no one else had started attacking yet, but she didn't plan to push her chances on that.

As the man swung around she delivered a sharp kick to his midsection, doubling him over. She rolled over the top of the man, so that she once again faced the army with her ship at her back and then used a firm boot to the man's raised backside to send him sprawling into the ground.

"So, this is just like, a test right? I pass?"

The man stood. As he did, two more officers moved forward and placed their hands on his shoulders. As they did, Heather noted the links passing from the men to her opponent, adding more souls to his disposal.

The man nodded again, then moved, this time with the speed of lightening. She barely managed to parry. Her reflexes kicked in, however and she followed the parry around with another kick.

It felt like she connected with the side of a tree. The sudden sturdiness of her opponent caused her to drop her guard. She barely managed to recover enough to avoid being skewered by an upswing of the man's khopesh. It sliced a small layer of her skin off of her left arm, leaving a burning sensation that told her the blade wasn't entirely normal.

Heather dropped all pretense of showing off and focused on not losing. The man moved quickly, but she remained a hair faster. This time, when he brought his sword down she stepped into it, using her crossed blades to redirect its energy. She used the momentum to spin the man a half step to the side. It sped through just enough to pass his guard and without taking a chance, Heather slide her left blade up through the man's ribs and into his chest.

To her surprise, six of the other soldiers doubled over and fell to the ground. She pulled her blade out and stepped back. The officer stood and stared at her coldly once more. The last two officers came forward, again passing their links to her opponent. As they did, the cut in the man's side sealed shut.

"This seems hardly fair. You keep drinking souls between rounds, and I don't get so much as a Gatorade?"

The last round had been close. Too close. With that much extra power, Heather didn't like the odds that she could win if she continued to observe the rules of this land. That left two options. Lose, or break the rules.

"There's no such thing as a fair fight." She reminder herself. One of the first rules she had learned upon coming to this side. "If there were, nobody would win."

Her opponent shifted his stance, indicating, as he had before, that the final round was about to commence. The moment before he moved to attack, Heather shifted her position fifty feet to her left, placing herself in the middle of one of the phalanxes of Egyptian soldiers. Before they could register what she had done, she attacked. As fast as she could manage in this land, she whirled her blades in a deadly tornado. The men didn't stand a chance.

As her opponent turned to try to register what she had done, Heather shifted her position again to another point in the battle, this time dropping another twenty men.

If these men were the source of her opponent's power, then she would just have to whittle that power down to something more manageable. Heather shifted again. This time her opponent stood waiting. She suspected he would catch on before too long, but she'd hoped to drop at least one more phalanx. The man attacked in his one blur, but her pre-emptive strikes must have done damage. His speed fell in line with what he had been during their last bout.

Heather parried his blade into one of his own men. Here in the middle of his energy source, she had the advantage. Bystanders were an acceptable target for her, while any one that he dropped removed more energy from his own attacks.

She employed the death of a thousand cuts. Perhaps less honorable than the man deserved, but Heather had long since realized that honor was a luxury one only had when they either had a death wish or significantly more power than their opponent. Right now, she possessed neither.

The damage showed results. The man had landed a few slices against her that stung far worse than they should, but he quickly slowed down to a speed where she could comfortably counter attack. A few more soldiers, and she might actually gain back the advantage.

The man feinted to the left, but Heather saw it coming a mile away. She sidestepped, but as he went to swing backwards, Heather shifted herself again to his flank. The move caught him off guard, and Heather took her opportunity to swing high at his exposed neck.

She had expected to feel the sensation of her sword passing through the man's neck, likely lopping his head clean off. What she instead found was confusion. At some point, somehow, she had managed to move into a kneeling positions with both swords stuffed blade down into the ground next to her.

Heather looked up in alarm, half expecting to see her attacker preparing to strike. Instead, a smile met her from a women who looked like an almost clichéd version of Cleopatra.

"Hello, Heather. So wonderful to see you."

Chapter 14

"Now, Jacob. She's as distracted as she's going to get."

Jacob nodded to Jack's disembodied voice then proceeded to walk up the docks. As had become usual, everyone he encountered moved out of his way without apparently realizing why or even that they were doing so.

It was weird, being alone among people. And not entirely a bad thing. Jacob had grown up in a overcrowded world where privacy was a luxury. Combine that with the feeling of never being truly accepted for himself, and he'd grown quickly to dislike being around others. When he had died, he'd awoken in his version of paradise, a large empty world without another soul insight.

It really felt like heaven, at least for a while. But after a while the loneliness began catching up with him. Luckily, Jack chose that point to show up and offer him the job. His life after death had marked the first time had had been able to just be himself and be accepted for it.

But even then, he still needed to escape and recharge. This new existence oddly suited him. He walked alone among everyone. There were many others to watch and listen to, but no one asked him questions. No one interfered with him. He could do his job and move on without explanation.

Today, his job changed dramatically. Ever since he'd awoken, Jack had had him playing the Angel of Death. The council stood on edge. They needed a push to get them over the cliff. Jacob came here to the docks to provide that push.

His targets came into view ahead of him. Ten Egyptians unloaded their cargo, while another in priest gear looked on. Jacob stopped as the Priest looked up in his direction. For a moment, inexplicably, it seemed the man could see him. Then his gaze shifted, and Jacob let his guard fall back.

"Must have been looking at something behind me." He told himself.

Just to be on the safe side, Jacob took a longer path around, keeping as much out of direct view as possible. Jack's plan was as solid as it could be, but even he had admitted to Jacob that he did not know the extent of Set's power, or what she passed on to her priests. Jack shared near infinite power with others. Set held it all herself, and had done so for centuries now.

Jacob studied the group of foreigners. As Jack had told him, all of the workers seemed to be directly linked to the Priest. This probably made controlling them much easier. Set issues a command to the Priest, the Priest then issues it out to the others with no dissent in the ranks. But it also made them more vulnerable. This was something that likely hadn't been an issue since the holy war ended, which Jacob counted on for lowering their guard.

Jacob would have preferred more time to make this happen, but he also knew that Heather was currently keeping the God of the Egyptians busy. While she did have an amazing gift for causing distractions, Jacob didn't want to push that window of opportunity any more than he had to.

The moment he saw the Priest turn back towards the far end of the peer, Jacob made his move. In a swift motion he materialized his black blade and closed the distance to the Priest. If the man had been able to see or hear him, he showed no mention of it. The moment he came within reach, Jacob slashed the blade.

The results were chaotic. The ten men and women under the control of the Priest all dropped their boxes and pulled weapons, spinning for an enemy. The movement caught the locals off guard, and old prejudices kicked in as people automatically assumed they were the targets. Most ran, a few pulled weapons and charged the sailors, who defended themselves appropriately.

The Priest stepped back, obviously trying to make sense of what happened to him. Jacob didn't give him much time to contemplate it as he grabbed a connection from his own shoulder and slammed it into the Priest.

Jacob had hoped the Priest would welcome the connection just as the souls he'd been collecting since his "rebirth". He really hadn't expected it to be the case though, and the Priest immediately confirmed those thoughts, pushing back against the connection, attempting to keep it from syncing completely.

"Who are you?" He demanded, his face visibly contorting as he concentrated on keeping the link from overpowering him.

"Just a man doing a job." Jacob pushed mentally, struggling to bring the man under control. He could feel the confusion radiating up through the sailors under his control as they fought to defend themselves from the many different Greeks on the docks taking the opportunity to strike back at their long distrusted ancient enemies.

They were far stronger than the Greeks but the Greeks had numbers and the Priest's struggles were spilling back to them, slowing their pace. They weakened visibly, and each one that did made his struggle against the priests slightly easier.

"Lady Set will never stand for this treachery." The priest grumbled, falling to one knee.

"Yeah." Jacob replied, standing straighter. "I think that's probably part of the point." As another sailor fell to the mob, the priest's will snapped. His eyes went blank as Jacob seized complete control of him and the sailors. The connection was still not very stable, but he didn't need it to be. Their current forms wouldn't last very long. "Now. Go reinforce their fears."

The Priest stood without question, then turned with a blood curling war cry to Set and charged into the fray. Most of the Greeks fell back at the site, but quickly determined that the unarmed Priest could be overwhelmed. More joined the fray, and within seconds it ended in a bloody massacre.

Jacob assimilated most of the energy from the falling sailors, pouring the rest into his blade. The crowd around him screamed a combination of defiance, anger, victory and racial slurs. Already he could see Egyptians on other docks frantically racing towards their boats as the crowd decided to repeat its victory.

It was as ugly as Jack had predicted it would be. And Jacob had started it. Not one of his prouder moments, but it was done.

"You better be right about this being worth it, Jack."

His leader didn't respond, but it didn't really matter. Word would spread quickly to everyone. This job completed, others now called him. Death never took a holiday.

Chapter 15

"**Y**ou may stand up now."

Heather stood without hesitation. It disturbed her almost as much as finding herself kneeling in the first place had. She had to fight to re-establish what felt like control of her own body. The link directly to Jack and his power helped, but even with that she struggled not to want to do everything she could to please the woman in front of her.

"Set, I suppose?"

"It's as good a name as any. It's good to see you, again."

Jack had warned her that Set had apparently absorbed the souls of many of their lost cohorts. "Yeah, I would say the same, except I'm not sure who all you are."

Set shrugged her shoulders and began walking. "Isn't that the nature of being a god?" Heather followed her without even thinking about it. "I'm everyone. And I am no one. My memories are vast and the lives I have lived and still live, quite varied. I called you friend in some, stood as your enemy in others. In most I've never met you but in enough you stick out as someone I cared for."

"Well." Heather considered, trying to figure out how to respond or what the woman expected of her. "Thanks, I guess?"

"That does not mean I would not recycle you in a moment if you do not answer my questions, despite what tricks Jack no doubt believes he has in place to protect you."

Heather wanted to believe that the woman was bluffing, but all evidence pointed to the contrary. The Goddess's very presence disconcerted her. Heather reconsidered her earlier beliefs. Meeting her end at the hands of this god no longer seemed quite so cool. Still, Set had not ended her yet, so if she played along then she might still manage to escape this mess with her soul intact. "Yeah. Well, I guess that's sort of why I'm here."

"Excellent. What does Jack want?"

"To go home." Heather replied without a beat.

"A worthy goal. One I have all but given up on. What is his plan?"

Heather shook her head. "He did not share it with me." A true statement so far as she could tell She had gaps in her memories of the private meetings that she had with Jack. There were apparently things he had stripped from her mind, somehow. Now that she considered it, that felt kind of creepy. "At least, not that I can remember, anyway."

Set nodded. "Of course. No reason to give me incentive to take your mind for details that wouldn't be there. But I'm sure you have some pieces. He would want to intrigue me, after all."

Heather shrugged. "Something to do with a link he believes he can re-establish with the other side. But I don't know how, or why."

"And if I were to just take his soul?"

"He doesn't think you could, but I suspect that even if you did, the link would be destroyed. I can't sense any of my links, after all, so I guess you've got to be top dog for it to work? Maybe?"

Set stopped, and looked out over the ocean, obviously pondering something. Her face contorted for a brief moment, as if she had some thought she disliked, but it passed just as quickly and her look resumed its placid expression once more. "And what does he want from me?"

"Optimally, he would like for you to join to him. He's certain he could bring down the Glacier if you do. Barring that, he wishes you to stay out of his way."

Set's eyes narrowed as she turned her eyes back to Heather. "You mean don't spoil his charade as he uses me as a boogie man to bring those fools on his council to heel?" The woman smiled, but there was no warmth in it. "He's played his part well. I suspect that even if I were to personally attempt to expose his plan, it would only reinforce those fools' distrust of me. So be it."

Heather, once again, found herself inadvertently dropping to her knees. Set towered over her, a terrifying visage of power immeasurable. For the first time, perhaps since her death, Heather genuinely felt afraid. She was a mosquito next to this woman, and whether or not she continued to exist or witnessed her own soul become shredded beyond measure was very obviously of little consequence.

"Understand this." The woman's voice dug into the depths of her brain, setting her entire being aflame. "I remember what it was to be a slave. To have my body used for the pleasure of others in life, my mind and soul reduced to fuel for someone else's desire in death. I will never again kneel to another, man or woman. If Jack makes one genuine move against me, I will destroy him and everything else on the other side of this River. All of you will burn."

Heather realized she had curled up in the sand in a near fetal position. She tried to reduce her own whimpering, but had no control to do so. She watched helplessly as the god turned her view back to the boat Heather had arrived on. In a blink it erupted in flames of black. Screams echoed for a few moments from its deck, and to her further horror Heather recognized each of the voices of those who had travelled with her.

The flames dissipated in moments, leaving the husk of the boat she had journeyed on to begin a slow descent into the River.

Set turned back to her. "I'll overlook his attack on my people this time, since he was kind enough to send me replacements for the souls he reaped. But tell him not to let such an event happen again. I might not be so forgiving next time."

She turned, dismissively calling back over her shoulder. "I'll withdraw my remaining sailors. That will reinforce the prejudices of those morons who serve Jack. Say hello to him for me, and do take as long as you need to pull yourself together before you signal him to pull you back. "

She sat down on a throne, which a contingent of shirtless slaves immediately picked up. They began moving in the direction of the large pyramid, followed by all of the remaining soldiers.

Within moments, only the curled whimpering form of Heather and a few dead bodies remained.

Heather fought to regain her composure. It took far longer than she would ever admit.

Chapter 16

"Team, this is Shantae." Thomas said as the two returned to Leo's plateau. Marcus had already resumed his female appearance. Thomas saw no reason to go into further explanation of the woman's other identity. If she wanted them to know, she could share that piece of her. "Shantae, this is Cho, and Leo."

"So these are our ragtag saviors of the underworld, huh?" Shantae smiled as she nodded to each one.

"Most of what is left." Thomas replied. "Has Buster returned?"

He knew the answer, but felt better asking it aloud.

"No, Friend Thomas." Cho replied.

That seemed strange. Thomas had expected, or at least hoped, that the dog's mission would have been quick. He could still feel his friend out there, with an edge of concern coming through the link, but so far the German shepherd had not encountered any serious danger. Thomas resisted the urge to probe the dog's thoughts for more details. It was extremely difficult to have access to people's thoughts and still respect their privacy.

"The gift of sight," Leo said, returning the conversation to Shantae, "You believe she has it then?"

"That is what I am told." Thomas replied, leaving off the part about who told him. Leo already knew and he saw no reason to bring the subject up with Shantae standing there. "But I was hoping you could confirm that. You're the only one who knows how it's supposed to work. I don't really even know what I would be explaining to her."

Leo nodded. "I can. It will take time."

Shantae smiled, "I'm a fast learner."

"Of this, I am glad to hear." Leo smiled. "But training a skill I do not personally possess to someone who has never seen it still takes time.

"Time is something we may not have enough of." Thomas lamented to himself. No point in bringing the subject back up aloud. Everyone here knew they were sitting on a bomb that could explode at any moment. Coughlin could make his final move at any time, and they were nowhere near ready. He had no idea how many souls would need to be reaped to fill the soul stone and make the blade they needed to stand a chance of defending themselves, but they were certainly not there yet.

"There is another way."

Thomas had grown used to Senebkay's sudden appearances. He had not, however, explained the strange Pharaoh to Shantae, so he made no physical reply to the spirit, instead raising an eyebrow.

Senebkay took the hint (or perhaps would have kept talking regardless, Thomas could never be certain). "You are sharing your link with this Shantae. You can share memories too. Give her the memories of your cohorts who have seen this power in action. It will be far easier for her to mimic them when she knows what it is supposed to look like."

Thomas agreed. "Leo, may I speak with you?"

"Of course." The small Italian nodded, then turned back to their new guest "Please excuse us."

Leo and Thomas walked over towards little hut Leo kept. It occurred to Thomas that he had never actually seen the Italian inside it.

"What is it you wish to discuss, Thomas?"

"There is a way that we can speed up the training of our new recruit. But it will require a sacrifice from you."

The Italian stood a bit straighter. "This sacrifice, what is it?"

"Your personal memories. I can pass them directly from you to her. I'll try and limit them to just your experiences with people like Heather who can do what you're asking her to do, but I can't promise that some other memories won't transfer too."

Leo's forehead wrinkled, the only visible shift of the considerations going on within his head. Thomas decided to give him all of the time he felt he needed. This would greatly speed up their progress, but he did not want to force the man into doing something he wasn't comfortable with, and he couldn't imagine many people being comfortable with having their memories Xeroxed and passed around.

After a few minutes of silence, the Italian nodded. "This plan, Thomas. I do not like it. But it has merit. I ask that you keep it minimal. But I will do as I must."

"Thank you, Leo." Thomas smiled. "Your help continues to be invaluable."

Thomas led the smiling but obviously nervous Italian back to where Cho and Shantae were standing and talking. Thomas quickly explained the plan to Shantae, who looked more intrigued than anything else.

"And this is a one way transfer, right?" She asked, suddenly slightly nervous.

"Yes." Thomas nodded. "Your privacy remains as much of your own as I can manage, just as I promised."

"Alrighty. Let's do this thing then."

Thomas nodded, and then grew a bit more solemn. "This is your last opportunity to walk away. In order to do this, I'll need to have you linked to me. Once that happens, you're in until this is over. Are you still willing to proceed?"

"Told you I was. "

"Good." Thomas nodded again. "Now please, turn around."

Shantae did so with what sounded like a sarcastic comment under her breath. Thomas didn't hear her. It would probably be the last time he didn't hear a comment she directed towards him, even if she were trying to hide it. With his own deep breath to calm himself, he once again reached into his shoulder and pulled out a link. The process was becoming more and more easy for him. That worried him somewhat. Without hesitation, he fixed the other end firmly to Shantae's shoulder just above where the blade would have been. The boost of new power, addictively sweet, rushed through his veins as he fought to keep the influx of new thoughts and memories from fully entering his mind.

"Dude. That is weird."

"Yes." Thomas agreed. It never ceased to be. He hoped it never did.

The process completed. For better or worse, Thomas now had another Soul under his belt, and Shantae was now locked into The Order of the Shield. No turning back now for either of them. Thomas briefly lamented having taken another step on this road against his will then pushed it out of mind. This was for his daughter. If it kept her safe, then he would pay any price demanded of him.

"Now that this is done, the memory transfer process, Thomas." Leo said, getting straight to this. "How does it work?" The man's anxiety showed clearly, and Thomas couldn't tell if he had more interest in knowing about it or just getting it over with.

"Put your hand on both of their shoulders." Senebkay told him. "It will make it easier for you to concentrate."

"Shantae, please turn back around. Leo, stand next to her."

Both did as he asked, and Thomas, for his part, placed his hand on each of their shoulders.

"Tell Leo to focus only on the memories he wishes to transfer. When he has done so, scan his surface thoughts and share them with Shantae."

"Leo, I need you to lock away everything you wish to keep secret, then concentrate on all of the examples you can think of for what Shantae needs to master. Ready?"

When Leo nodded, Thomas opened a channel directly between the two and began transferring the surface memories over. The images flickered in rapid secession in his own mind as they passed over, copied like files from one computer to another. Thomas hoped that they were of more use to Shantae than they were to him.

Granted, he wasn't keeping them in his own mind and building off of them, but still, they had all the training power for him of flipping through someone's photo album.

"Wait." Shantae cried out, and suddenly the image froze on a shot of Heather slicing what looked to be a cord connecting someone to a sanctuary while Jacob punched a shadowing figure that lunged at her. "Who..." her voice stumbled, as if she were afraid to complete the question. "Who is that."

"Heather." Leo replied, a bit visibly strained from separating memories. "She is the most recent example on our team of someone with your abilities."

"NO!" Shantae screamed excitedly. "Behind her. The man!"

"That would be Jacob."

Shantae broke Thomas's grip, stumbling backwards. Shock, disbelief, hope, anger, love, sorrow and a wealth of other emotions rolled off of her too loudly for Thomas to shut out.

"Where is he? Is he... is he gone?"

Thomas suddenly remembered back to their first meeting together, where Marcus confided that there was only one person he wished to find on this side of death. "He's the one, isn't he? The person you hoped to find in the afterlife."

Shantae nodded, a wave of fear overpowering the other emotions.

"There's still hope, Shantae. I told you that some of our companions were trapped in another place. Jacob is one of them. As far as we know, they are safe there. Part of what we are trying to find is a way to bring them back."

Shantae nodded again, wiping away tears from her eyes. "Then I will do absolutely everything to help you. Name it. No questions asked."

Thomas nodded. So this is why Capone had been so certain he would be able to talk Marcus into helping them. "Good. I promise we'll do what we can to get Jacob back. Now, should we continue with what we were doing?"

Shantae shook her head. "No. I told you I'm a fast study. I think I can do this. At least enough to get started."

Leo cocked his head. "The abilities we need, you think you can wield them?" Thomas could feel the relief coming off of him, mixed with a tinge of disbelief.

"Yeah." Shantae nodded. "It's like the Matrix. There is no spoon."

Leo cocked his head with confusion. "This reference. I do not understand it."

"It means this whole place is fake." Shantae explained. "We see what we see, but if we look behind it, we can see the code that makes it up. Mess with that code and you change the place."

Leo nodded. "That is true, I think. It makes as much of a sense as I think it can be put."

"Good." Thomas added. "Then put it to the test, shall we? Leo, put us back on the plane."

"This plan, do you think it is wise?"

"No." Thomas added honestly. He wished there were more time to take it slow, but he feared every moment wasted would haunt them soon. "But if we play it safe, Coughlin will win. We're going to have to take some risks. "

Thomas could tell by the look on Leo's face that he understood that, even if he didn't like it.

"Very well." He nodded quietly. "I will open the pool."

Chapter 17

Thomas took stock of his surroundings and immediately hated it. He was back on the too cramped plane once more. This time he found himself in the middle of two recognizable passengers.

Shantae was to his left with a window seat. Cho was to his right sitting next to the aisle.

"Well, at least we're all together this time."

"That was me." Shantae smiled proudly. "Told you I was a quick study!"

Thomas nodded. That was certainly a better start. "Great! Now can you take control of this thing and find out who we're fighting?"

Shantae twisted her lips. "Hopefully. But that's going to take time. Think of it kind of like hacking a website. Modifying some of the existing code is way easier than rewriting the code completely."

"Do your best. We'll see if we can buy you some time. Cho, take the aisle. This may be far more noticeable than last time."

Shantae closed her eyes, apparently concentrating on the task that only she could currently see. Cho unfastened his seatbelt and stood up, keeping an eye in both directions for trouble.

Thomas marveled for a brief moment at how easily he was taking to giving orders these days, then moved his mind back towards the situation at hand. He unfastened his own belt and stood up, stretching his already cramped legs.

"Some extra room would help us."

"I can do that." Shantae nodded. Within a few seconds, the distance between the seats seemed noticeably wider.

"Nice work." Thomas was impressed. He hated to admit he was wrong, but he could already see why the team had pressured him to take another soul on. If Shantae could master this, then their path to filling the stone would be far quicker.

"I've got good news and bad news." Shantae said, suddenly sounding more serious than before. "Good news is that I think I can unravel this nightmare. Bad news is that I can't do it quietly. I'm sure there's a way to do so but if there is, I ain't got the experience to pull it off. I'm pretty sure that if I do one more thing, I'm going to alert everyone here to what we're up to."

"So, this is the point of no return."

"Yep. Pretty much."

"Cho? You ready?"

The Asian man slid one leg backwards, taking a stance that would allow him to quickly change directions in the narrow aisles. "Ready, Friend Thomas."

Thomas nodded. "Welcome to the team, Shantae. Here's where you earn your place."

Shantae, eyes still closed, gave a single quick nod. "You got it, boss."

As if on queue, the plane rocked as if it had hit turbulence, and the "Please Fasten Your Seat Belt" sign dinged on.

Thomas braced himself. "Here we go."

"Sir, you're going to need to sit down." Thomas didn't notice the flight attendant approaching, but suddenly she was on the other side of Cho, pointing a stout finger towards his seat.

"I'm afraid I need to stand, ma'am."

A large man stood up behind Cho, his head tipped slightly to fit avoid hitting the top of the plane. "Are we going to have a problem here?"

"I'm afraid we might." Added the flight attendant, her eyes narrowing.

"Friend Thomas?" Cho asked.

Thomas had hoped to put this off until there was a better arena, but there appeared little more they could do to stall. "Do it, Cho."

Cho nodded, then with lightning speed landed a punch that sent the tall passenger flying backwards through the aisle, then side kicked the stewardess. Surprisingly, she only took a couple of steps backwards.

"Sir," The woman said, eyes narrowing. "You MUST take your seat."

"Ugh."

Thomas turned away from Cho's fight to see Shantae fumbling to unfasten her seatbelt. He could tell by the panicked look on her face that it was growing too tight. Thomas tried to assist, but the buckle was stuck fast, and the belt was not budging. He checked his pockets, but of course, had no sharp objects to slice it with.

Thomas attempted to create a knife, but it faded after just a glimpse of reality.

"That's against the rules of the world." Senebkay whispered in his mind. Thomas wasn't sure where the Pharaoh was currently hiding at, but he was obviously watching. "Do something unexpected. Catch them off guard."

Thomas immediately turned the seatbelt into a balloon. Obviously whomever was in control of the world did not think to stop such a thing from happening, because it snapped into its new shape as if it had always been that. Before it could be reverted, Thomas popped it.

"THANK YOU!" Shantae gasped, obviously catching her breath. Apparently breathing somehow factored into this sanctuary now.

"No problem!" Thomas replied. "Keep working!"

"HANDS IN THE AIR!"

Thomas spun to spot the new voice. As he did he tried to take in the remaining situation. Cho was still fighting the Flight attendant and the large passenger. The flight attendant had somehow procured a drink cart and was attempting to run Cho down with it. Judging by the sounds of impact it made when he fought it off it was far heavier than any normal cart would be. The large passenger was more of a nuisance than anything else, the small aisle preventing his bulk from being used to much advantage.

The new voice belonged to a man dressed as an air marshal. His side arm was pulled and pointed directly at Thomas.

"Whoa! It was just a balloon popping."

"I SAID HANDS IN THE AIR!"

Thomas wanted to morph into his cat form and attack, but the layout did not appear conducive to that. The tight quarters meant his big cat form would be just as hindered as the large passenger. His normal fallback, a fireball, seemed just as poor of a choice. He had no idea what a blast of fire would do in this contained area.

"Look, I was just trying to help my friend here and..."

The marshal ("is he real, or an automaton?" Thomas wondered) appeared to have had enough talk and opened fire, letting three shots fly from the gun.

Thomas instinctively raised his hand to slow them down as he had back in Shantae's bar. For a split second it worked, but then the bullets continued on their trajectory. Thomas realized he wouldn't be able to stop them here without pulling substantial power from the other souls linked to him, but he could deflect them. So he did, edging the path of the bullets towards the side of the plane where they pierced the side.

"Well, that probably wasn't a good plan for either of us." Thomas thought as lights shifted to red and masks fell from the ceiling. Thomas lost site of the air marshal as he tumbled backwards into his chair at the rocking turbulence. Even Cho seemed to be struggling to hold his footing.

"Soon would be good, Shantae." Thomas called out as he tried standing back up.

"I'm working on it!" She screamed back.

Thomas felt the tubes of the oxygen masks snake around him as if they were alive. He yanked against them, pulling some out, but others seemed to take their place. There were at least fifteen masks dangling in his seating area, and each of their tubes seemed to grasp for him.

In his struggles, Thomas caught a glimpse of Cho fly past him, apparently having been caught off guard by the attacking drink cart. The stewardess was charging towards him, pushing the cart like it was a steamroller intent on flattening him. Thomas threw a screw up in the floor, tall enough to catch the wheels of the cart and stop them fast, its momentum causing the cart to flip and sending the flight attendant sprawling into a group of alarmed passengers.

Cho for his part slid back so that he was out of the way of the crashing cart, which instead rolled into the large passenger. Cho took the chance to leap to his feet, turning back towards the flight attendant.

To Thomas's surprise, the woman merely smiled and sat in a now empty seat, fastening her own belt.

"Ladies and Gentlemen" A male voice came on the loud speaker. "We will be experiencing some turbulence. Please take your seat and observe the Fasten Seatbelt sign."

Before Thomas could react he felt a rush of air behind him. "Oh crap."

The small bullet holes suddenly merged together, and half of the side of the plane ripped away.

"CRAP. " Thomas screamed as he held tightly to his seat, merging his feet with the floor of the plane to keep himself literally planted. Cho flew backwards but caught himself on the edge of the plane's wall, feet hanging off into the freezing night sky as the air screamed over everyone.

Shantae had managed to wrap her arms around her armrests for now and used that to continue in her seat.

Thomas heard more of the plane's metal start to groan again and suddenly another chunk of the cabin peeled away, taking the ceiling above him with it.

For a brief moment, the scene shifted and he was standing in a quiet park, then he was back in the plane, air screaming around him and the taut rubber tubes of the oxygen masks threatening to drag him off into the void with the piece of fuselage that they were attached to. Thomas started to turn into a mist, allowing the tubes wrapped tightly around him to slip harmlessly through him, but then he spotted Cho flopping from the side of the metallic cabin piece like a flag in a stiff breeze.

If Thomas let the piece fly away, Cho would go with it. He redoubled his grip, fighting against the force of the kite-like piece of metal threatening to drag him out. He could feel his feet slide back, letting loose of the floor, taking much of his stability with it. He wasn't going to last long.

"This is not going well." Senebkay's voice rang in his ear.

"Tell me something I don't know." Thomas replied, annoyed at the unhelpful interruption.

"You will potentially return to the River if you do not do something. Take in your lesser souls. Shift the balance. This rogue soul's barely holding her own against the three of you. Pull in all of your power and she doesn't stand a chance."

"NO!" Thomas screamed, as much to the situation as to Senebkay. He did not want to take in all of the souls attached to him. Not only would that be a severe violation of their trust in him, but it would also risk giving control back to the Pharaoh, and Thomas wasn't sure he could wrest that control back a second time.

But the Egyptian was right. Things were going poorly and all of them could die here. Or worse become trapped forever.

"We're going to have to get out of here if you can't get this done quickly, Shantae!"

"Almost there!"

Thomas considered his options. His grip was firm for the moment, but he was barely able to keep it there. Any changes in pressure might prove more than he could hold. He could pull Cho completely back into himself.

That still risked giving enough power that Senebkay could retake control, but it was better than losing his friend to the seemingly endless night sky.

"Ladies and gentlemen," The pilot's voice returned, more calm than he should have been given the gaping whole in his plane, "it looks like we're about to meet with some poor weather conditions. Please remain seated."

"Crap." Thomas shook his head. "This isn't worth it."

For another brief moment he caught a glimpse of a serene park around him, then the lightening crashed and a hard gust of wind threatened to pull him and Cho completely off into oblivion.

"Almost there!" Shantae screamed over the now howling wind , as hard drops of rain began to pelt the group.

"Too late." Thomas called out. This was better than last time, but still too dangerous. "I'm pulling the plug!"

Faced between losing a team member, potentially giving himself back to the Pharaoh, or calling it quits, Thomas had decided that discretion was the better option. He closed his eyes, and pictured all of them standing back at Leo's plateau. He felt the familiar energy gather around him.

Then it fizzled.

"Damn it. " He cried out. "They've locked us in."

Shantae nodded. "I see it."

"Can you undo it?"

Shantae shook her head. "Not easily!"

Hail began to pelt them. Thomas wanted to scream. He glanced back to see Cho still managing to hold onto the metallic plating that had once been the side of the plane, now completely detached save for the cords wrapped around and dragging at Thomas. He heard a cackle of laughter from the flight attendant.

She was the source of this, he was certain, but that did nothing to help him with what to do about it.

A bolt of lightening struck down at him. Thomas's training with Jack was enough that he managed to deflect it, but only barely. The smell of ozone ripped through his senses along with an uncomfortable electric tingling. He could feel his grip slipping.

"Take the damn souls in!" Senebkay's voice demanded. "Do not let your stubbornness get us recycled!"

Thomas grunted. He seriously pondered the pharaoh's option. He was almost certainly going to lose himself if he did, and his friends, but there was a chance that he could some day overcome Senebkay's will and reclaim their mind. If he did nothing, they might all be lost.

"Friend Thomas!"

Thomas looked back. Cho was hanging by one arm, trying desperately not to be shaken off of the storm tossed piece of metal. Thomas tried materializing some form of rope, but found he couldn't. He was apparently locked down.

Thomas reached out and took the silver cord leading to Cho. "I'm sorry, my friend."

The quiet caught Thomas off guard. It took a moment to realize that he was now standing on dew filled grass in a peaceful park. He glanced about to see that Cho, too, was as confused but safe as he. Shantae, however, was grinning from ear to ear.

"Told you I could do it!"

In the distance, children ran and played. Behind him, he saw the stewardess, looking as bewildered as Cho. Slightly beyond her stood a tall man in a pilot's uniform, looking at the flight attendant in slight confused recognition.

"Brenda?"

"Take them both, now." Senebkay whispered in his ear. "While they're still confused. It'll be easier."

The man stumbled over to the woman, who looked back at him in a combination of anger and embarrassment. "Brenda, what did you do?"

"Take them now, Thomas!"

Thomas shook his head, still not seeing the Pharaoh in body. "Not yet. I need to see where this goes."

Senebkay's voice showed frustration. "Think of the stone! You need souls to fill it! Do it!"

"You left me, Charles!" The woman, Brenda, Thomas assumed, whimpered. "You left me for her!"

"I remember." The man nodded slowly, as if coming out of a stupor. "And you... you killed yourself?"

The woman turned away, not answering.

"Why would you have killed yourself? We weren't even that happy together."

The woman's voice was barely audible. "You left me."

"How.... wait.... I died too, didn't I? That's how you're here. But when.... Why was I flying our plane? I haven't been on that in two years. But..."

The woman collapsed, burying her head in her hands and sobbing. The man, Charles, merely stood and watched in confusion. Thomas decided it was time for some clarification.

"You are dead, Charles. This is your afterworld. Or it should have been, but Brenda here hijacked it, and molded it to fit her desire instead of yours."

The man looked down, still not completely grasping what was going on. "Brenda? Is that true?"

The woman looked up at him, tears staining her face. "I'm sorry. I just wanted... I wanted us...." She shook her head. "I'm sorry."

And she was gone.

"Still time to go after her." Senebkay voiced helpfully.

Thomas ignored her, and turned back to Shantae. "Any trace of her in this sanctuary?"

The black woman shook her head. "Nope. All gone. She let go of all control."

"Good." Thomas nodded, then turned back to Charles. "You're in control now. Practice, and you can make it look like you want. Now that you know, it'll be really hard for her to come back if you don't want her too."

"Can I..." the man started. "Can I go see her? I think I owe her an apology."

Thomas thought that they might be considered even, all things considered, but he did not know the two's history. "If she doesn't mind. That doorway..." he pointed to the shimmering gate a few yards from where they were. "That will take you back to the 'Real world'. We call it the 'Prime'. Find the location where she died and you'll be able to find a similar entrance to hers. But only if she lets you in. "

"Thank you." The man nodded.

"If she comes back, we'll be here to deal with her. I hope it goes with out saying that the same would apply to you if you tried taking over her sanctuary without her approval."

Charles shook his head. "I won't. And I doubt she will either. She was hurt. Worse than I thought she would be apparently. But I'll talk to her. I know her. She won't try to hurt me."

"Right." Thomas shrugged. "Well then. We'll be leaving."

With that he turned and pictured his friends transporting back to Leo's. As he did, he felt a bit of disappointment coming from Senebkay.

"Well. That was a total waste of our time."

In terms of filling the stone, the man was probably right. But overall, this had been very productive. Shantae had jumped in as if she had experienced the usual training period, and had exceeded his expectations by far.

There would be other rogue souls. Ones dangerous enough to justify returning them to the River. The stone would be filled. For the first moment in some time, Thomas was beginning to feel hopeful.

Chapter 18

"What happened here?" Crisa asked with concern as she appeared in the throne room.

Jack was honestly surprised that it took her as long as it did, and that no one else had arrived. It proved that they had no power to spy on him, else the attack would have certainly drawn them in.

Jack pointed to the three dead Egyptian bodies laying near the throne. "A test, I'm guessing."

Crisa looked confused. "Set sent three assassins to attack a god? I can see where she would be able to sneak them in, but the moment they attacked, they wouldn't stand a chance."

"Nor did they," Jack agreed. "But I wasn't the target. At least, not my actual person." He pointed behind Crisa to a figure she had missed. Darius, the former Persian King, sat in contemplation at the other end of the Throne room. He was literally surrounded by Greek hoplites. "Can you sense him?"

Crisa's eyes widened. "No. But... how can..."

Jack pointed at his head. "Their target was the helm. Or, rather, the connection to the crown. The three of them appeared and struck in concert at one of the connections. I destroyed them immediately, but not before the damage was done. When I realized who it was that was missing I brought him here and put him under enough guard that he could not be picked off."

Jack sighed and shook his head. "I honestly don't think she knew or cared which of you she was severing, she just wanted to know if it would work. Or let us know that she'd exposed a weakness that she could exploit. Who knows?"

"This is very disturbing." Crisa said with a shutter.

In the months that Jack had dealt with the woman, he'd never noted anything to truly concern her. This did. "Good." He thought. But he kept that thought masked, instead putting his own face of concern forward. "Agreed. If she had known which of you she had been going to sever..."

"...She could have acted fast enough to take all of the souls attached to that person." Crisa finished. "Gods. It would only take one or two strikes like that to tip the scales of power completely in her favor."

Jack shook his head. "We can't let that happen. I'll have to create a personal guard around me at all times. Slow them down enough that I can eliminate them before they strike."

Crisa nodded, but her face grew more concerned. "That's a start, but it may not be enough. All she'd have to do is sacrifice a slightly larger strike force. If she loses fifty souls and can gain a thousand in return, she would. Of that I've no doubt."

"I don't know what else to do, lass. I could protect the connections made directly to me better, but it's bad enough having me own mates floating about my head. I really don't want all of your minds bumbling about there as well."

"I know." Crisa nodded. "Nor would the council be thrilled about the prospect. But there's a small chance we all lose that choice."

"What about him." Jack pointed at Darrius. "Can we repair his connection? I don't think he wants to spend the next thousands years having one of us watching him twenty four seven. "

Crisa shook her head. "I... I don't know. It took us months to make the helm, and more souls than I care to count. I'm not really even sure what souls we got the ideas from."

Jack knew. Several of the souls responsible had since been discarded to the underworld. Jack had stumbled across the knowledge of the helm's creation, and the costs involved, some time ago. It's the reason he'd started this plan to begin with.

But again, he kept that knowledge buried, instead adding "Well, if we can't get him connected back to the helm, we'll need him to join with one of you. He may not like it, but it'll be a site better than leaving all of his souls open to Set."

Crisa nodded. "This should be discussed with all. I'll call the council."

"THIS IS OUTRAGEOUS!" Argos boomed. Jack could always count on the big warrior to use any justification for violence. "We cannot let this go unpunished."

The statesman Mikon looked over at the big man, with a rare bit of visible annoyance. "Quit your blustering, Argos. You know as well as we do that a direct assault at this point would accomplish little."

Jack thought it interesting just how shaken the normally composed man was. If the stress of this impending war was getting to him, it was a good sign.

Mikon continued. "We need to determine two things. What do we do with Darius, and is there a way to better protect the helm?"

"So that wench's actions will be allowed to stand?" Argos blustered in complete disbelief.

"None of us like this, hopolite." Golnar purred softly. "But Set is nothing if not cautious. She would not attempt such a thing without a clear advantage to gain. Until we know her mind, it is foolish to let rage guide us."

"Bah." Argos spat. "Rage gives one power."

"If I recall correctly, that line of thinking is what originally got you killed."

"Correct!" The big warrior laughed. "But it was a glorious death and I took countless enemies with me."

Mikon raised an eyebrow, "Except Set doesn't care how many of her minions you take with you. And if you fall to her, you become hers. Remember what she did to King Horatus during the Soul Wars?"

The big warrior didn't reply this time, and Jack was surprised to see a look of horror pass over the man's eyes. He made a note to himself to follow up on the story later and to see what it was that could scare the fearless man so.

The former Spartan king Teleklos took the break in conversation as a chance to move things forward. "As much as I too want to see vengeance repaid, I agree that now is not the time. It will come, Argos. Trust in that."

The big warrior did not appear mollified, but must of recognized if the Spartan king was not on his side, then odds were that he would be unable to bring others to agree with him.

"She will grow bolder, you mark my words. She will not stop until we stop her."

"Ye may very well be right, lad." Jack had been prepared to come in on whichever side of the argument needed to be balanced to keep the group near a stalemate. He had expected it would be that of the hot headed warrior. "I don't rightly like the idea of sitting about waiting for another strike team to set me in their sites. Even if we don't strike now, we should be preparing for some kind of attack to let her know this will not be tolerated. "

Teleklos nodded again. "Agreed. While the time is not yet nigh, it should be planned for. I will work with Argos and Golnar to identify potential areas where we can strike. It will need to be a large enough hit to let the Goddess know we are not to be trifled with, but not so large that it forces the war to start just yet.

Golnar studied the king for a moment, then looked back at Jack. "I will agree to this. It has been centuries since we've had such a challenge. Better that it be handled with finesse and planning."

Jack nodded. He would be interested to see what that trio came up with. "That sounds settled then. Now, the other question at hand: how do we best protect King Darius? And the souls he has. Can we have him re-attached to the Helm?"

"Not easily." It was the Greek statesman Mikon that replied. "I researched the topic recently, when you were added to our group. I wanted to know if, when you stepped down, we could easily add your soul to our numbers. The answer, I'm afraid, was not so promising. Most of the technique has been lost to centuries of recycling. The knowledge would have to be reassembled or recreated, and without knowing who held which parts of those souls now, such an undertaking would be most difficult."

Jack put on his best look of incredulousness. "None of ye bloody remember how you created this thing?"

"I'm afraid not." Mikon conceded. "I do not remember the details, but I seem to recall there being concern with the fact that knowing how to make the Helm could lead to knowledge on how to unmake the helm."

"It was a valid concern." This was added by Katina, who entered the room from the protected chamber that Darius and his massive guard regiment were currently occupying. "Remember, this was millennia ago, at the height of a war that still had multiple enemies and no certain outcome. There was also less trust in each other than we hold now. No single one of us would have been trusted by the group with knowledge that could have been used against the rest. And all of us knowing merely opened more of a risk of the knowledge falling into one of the other warring factions."

Jack nodded. He'd already known the end result, but it was interesting to know the reasons why it had come to be. He was glad he had centuries of these self-made gods being forced to work together behind them. There is little chance his plan would stand a remote chance of working if they were still as paranoid as they appear to have once been. "Very well. Makes sense. So odds of us recreating this technique?"

Mikon looked uncomfortable. "From scratch? Remote. But the memories still exist in our various souls. Finding them, however will be a problem unless..."

"No." The Spartan King Teleklos interjected calmly. "That's not happening, Greek. No point in discussing it."

Jack raised an eyebrow. "What exactly are we dismissing out of hand?"

"We could speed up the search by combining the memories. But as my companion King so quickly points out, that is easier said than done."

Jack nodded. This was the direction he wanted the conversation going. But he would have to play it carefully. "Combine the memories?"

The Spartan King looked even more annoyed. "He means we all pull in all of our souls. And if that doesn't work, we then give those souls, along with our own, to one of us long enough that that person to put the memories together."

"Aye. See where that would be tough to agree on."

"Yes." Crisa added. "That person would temporarily have access to all of the memories and all of the power of us all. If they chose that moment to not split everyone else back off.."

"They would be stuck will all of us in their heads." Jack interjected. "Not a bloody pleasant situation for them."

That made the both of the warriors bust out in laughter.

"Not everyone is as adverse to power as you, Jack Macintyre." Argos said with a smile. "Though I agree with you, having some of these contrarians in my head for even a second might prove too maddening."

Crisa shook her head at the laughter, and tried to keep the conversation on topic. "So we're not likely to recover the means of re-attaching Darius anytime soon. How do we protect him in the meantime."

"We attach him to one of us. " Teleklos added quickly. "It is the only other way."

Katina shook her head. "We could protect him, as we are right now. Keep a room sealed so that there's no teleporting in or out, then keeping constant guards."

"Too risky." Argos added, not surprisingly agreeing with Teleklos. "We would need to keep one of us focused on it twenty-four seven. Set could wait for a split second drop in attention and strike. Her gaining Darius's souls would be far more detrimental to us all, Darius included, than any one of us binding to him."

"As much as I hate to agree..." Mikon conceded, "I am afraid that I must. It is most safe this way. Hopefully Darius himself will agree, but even if he does not, we must do this. There is too much at risk to have his souls fall into Set's hands."

"Sounds like it is agreed them." Jack added, making sure to add a tinge of weariness to his voice. "Which one of you will be taking him on?"

"I'll take him." Teleklos added. "He was a fellow king in life. I'll see him taken cared for in death."

"Perhaps we should ask him?" Katina added. "While he's lost his spot on the Helm, he has still earned the right over the centuries to have his opinion heard."

Mikon nodded. "He should definitely have a vote, as always, but I do not believe we can allow his choice to be the sole factor. Again, the risks are too big. I, for one, would suggest that he be attached to the current Hades, Jack."

"Whoa now." Jack added quickly. "Let's not be hasty."

"I told you Jack," Crisa smiled, "It may not be your choice. I agree with Mikon. Jack's the logical choice. He's current Hades, and has shown with his own friend's souls that he can be trusted with allowing others to keep their autonomy."

To Jack's surprise, even Teleklos gave a cursory nod. "I still believe I would be the better choice. But I would support Jack Macintyre over others."

"Very well then." Katina sighed. "Let us bring in Darrius to see if he objects to this decision."

Chapter 19

"Wraiths." Senebkay spat. "Did not expect any of those to still exist."

Thomas listened to Buster's description of the soul he encountered in his search for the Great Spirit. It reminded him of how much he still had to learn about what was possible in the afterworld.

"What are these Wraiths?" he asked Senebkay. He often wondered how silly he looked having such conversations in front of the others, knowing they still could not see or hear the Egyptian.

"Just like Buster said. They're spirits cut off completely from their Sanctuary while they're in the Prime. They're left with no way to recharge, but the distance from the River means they don't actually just recycle back as they otherwise would. Instead they remain, becoming negative holes of energy."

Thomas translated to the others, who all listened intently.

"So pissed off ghosts." Shantae added. "Like some freaky horror movie."

Thomas nodded, and passed on more of what Senebkay added. "He says yes, and despite our already being dead, they're more scary."

"Damn." Shantae shook her head. "How are we gonna take on Freddy and the gang?"

"I have an idea." Senebkay replied. "But unless you're willing to bring me out to the others, we should discuss it in private."

Thomas nodded, then turned back to the others. "We don't know just yet, apparently. But I'll work on a plan. In the mean time, I want everyone practicing. We need to be as strong as possible if we're to get through this together."

The others agreed, and Cho and Shantae disappeared. Thomas traced their route and confirmed they had both gone to the training sanctuary, where Cho would no doubt continue testing Shantae's abilities.

Buster curled up on the ground and watched Thomas with a look of concern mixed with something else that Thomas couldn't entirely read. Leo mumbled to himself and returned to his pools.

'Okay." Thomas said, turning towards Senebkay. "What is your plan?"

"I've been going through everyone's memories."

"WHAT?" Thomas could barely contain his anger. "I told them we wouldn't do that!"

"No." Senebkay said patiently. "You told them YOU would not do that. Which was a stupid commitment."

"It's not stupid to respect people's privacy."

"It is when it will get everyone killed." The Pharaoh sighed. "We are at war, Thomas. One with many fronts. I have been through this before, and I can tell you the winner is NEVER the one who respects ANYTHING. Such sentiment, while seeming noble, is truly a weakness. If you care for these souls, or that of our daughter's, then you MUST stop pretending that there is any limit to what must be done to win."

Thomas shook with anger. He could not bring himself to agree with Senebkay's assessment, though a nagging part of him wondered if it might be true. Was he too nice for this job? He hadn't really wanted it to begin with. Was it worth winning if he had to become everything he despised? Could he afford to lose this though?

"THOMAS!" Thomas shook his head and looked up to see the Pharaoh glowering at him. "This is no time to second guess yourself. This is a time for action, and I know the path we must take."

Thomas blushed at being chastised, and then chastised himself for feeling ashamed of his misgivings. He was right. He knew he was. But for now it couldn't hurt to at least hear what the former god had to say. "Fine. What did these violations tell you?"

"We need souls to complete the stone and forge the soulblade."

"You didn't need to go snooping through other people's memories to learn that."

"No." Senebkay replied, clearing becoming frustrated. "But we know from our last outing that you are willing to sacrifice everyone for the sake of your conscious."

Thomas shook his head. "Those souls did not deserve to die. We couldn't just..."

"You could and you should have. It is either them or you, Thomas. You must remember that."

"NO!" The anger was barely containable. Thomas fought to regain control of his emotion. "No. I refuse to believe that."

Senebkay sighed. "I know. Which is why I went looking for another plan. And I found one. It's risky, but there seems little choice now."

Another plan. Thomas wasn't sure he wanted to hear it after everything else he'd heard so far, but he was forced to agree with Senebkay that time really was growing desperate. "Fine. What's this new plan?"

"We attack Coughlin's Hell."

Thomas stood confused, trying to wrap his mind around what exactly the Egyptian was proposing. "We.... Wait, what?"

"We attack Coughlin's Hell. The one he sat up for all of the horrible souls he captures. Memories of it were still stuck in the back of Leo's conscious. They're fragmented, but there is enough there that I can piece together what he's done and how he's doing it. "

"We attack Hell. Where we lost Jack and his band. The place we barely survived with a more seasoned team? Are you INSANE? No, of course you are. You'd have to be to..."

"THOMAS! Focus. Our options are limited. Do you want to save your daughter's world or not?"

Thomas shook his head. This was madness. "OF course I do but..."

"BUT NOTHING. Listen. Hear me out."

Thomas could only stare for a moment, trying to fathom how this could possibly turn into a good idea. In the end, his curiosity more than anything else forced him to give in. "Fine. What is this plan of yours?"

Thomas listened nervously as Senebkay revealed his ideas. After listening to it in full, he mulled over the proposal, as well as what the alternatives were. "I'll admit, it's.... less bad than I had expected. Still extremely risky..."

"But less so than our other options. Unless you're willing to expand your sacrifices to the stone."

Thomas shook his head. "No. You're right. The people Coughlin has caught.... They no doubt deserve death. It's better that way. Are you sure this can work?"

"Can? Yes. There's no doubt that it's possible. Will? That depends. But I'm confident enough in our odds to suggest it."

"We had better get to practicing then." The nagging voice in the back of his head told Thomas that this was stupid. He was asking too much of his team, and if they were caught...

But doing nothing was out of the question. Bad things were coming, and it was better to risk everything on a chance than to lose it all to wasted inactivity. Perhaps that was Senebkay's influence, but for now, he would allow it.

Chapter 20

Jack looked out his window and listened to the repetitive rhythm of the crashing waves. It used to be one of the most relaxing things he knew of. Its charmed diminished with each visit these days.

He felt trapped. The weight of the job he never wanted, the burden of the souls he never wished to carry, they remained a crushing load on his shoulders. He wanted a vacation. Whether it was a return to an old familiar place or a scouting mission to see something completely new didn't matter. So long as he was not here, he would embrace it.

But here was the only place he could be. That restriction annoyed him. He knew he shouldn't let it, but it did. There was just no way around it.

One way or the other, it would not be forever. He would not do as the souls that remained here for millennia had done. He would not accept this fate. He would either make his escape, or he would burn the whole thing to oblivion. He would become like the Chtullu mythos he enjoyed reading as a teen, a great old god sleeping at the edge of reality.

He couldn't decide for sure, honestly, which of those was more likely. The plans were proceeding as well as he could hope for, but there were far too many moving parts, far too many details for him to keep a close eye on. He was good at improvising to cover the mistakes and surprises, but would one come along that he couldn't handle? The possibility made him more nervous than he cared to admit, even to himself.

So deep in thought was he that it took him a moment to realize that the impossible occurred.

KNOCK *KNOCK* *KNOCK*

The sound, a firm and steady wrapping on the front door, startled him. The door, like the rest of this world, was a construct in his mind. There should be nothing here he had not created. And yet...

KNOCK *KNOCK* *KNOCK*

Jack froze, considering all of the endless, equally impossible, options that could have lead to someone else invading his most trusted sanctuary. None ended well. As the knock continued to get more persistent Jack began to draw on his considerable power, prepared to unleash everything the moment an attack happened, though he struggled to picture just what that attack might be. Finally, cautiously, he reached over and slowly pulled the door open.

"Jack, darling, no need for that." Set spoke nonchalantly as she sauntered past him. "I've no intention of fighting you here of all places, and any damage you did before I left would be temporary at best."

The Egyptian goddess wondered over to a wicker chair and stretched out in it as if she had been a common guest used to making herself at home. "Lovely place. It's nice to see actual water for a change. The pyramid's view is more spectacular but I've never completely grown used to the sea being such an odd color."

Jack closed the door and attempted to act more nonchalant than he felt. If Set could find her way in here, then there was a chance that she knew all of his plans. That put everything and everyone at risk. The only thing he could think to do was to play her game and hoped she showed more of her hand than she intended to.

"Lady Set. So lovely to see you too. Might I ask how you found your way here?"

"Of course you can ask, darling. You can also pour me a drink while you are at it. I seem to recall you being a connoisseur of beer. I remember liking the taste in several of my lives, but can never seem to get the flavor correct."

Jack shrugged, produced a couple of mugs of his favorite stout, then passed one onto her. "Fine. How did you get here?"

"You took some of my men. I've not yet worked out how you managed it, but in playing back the memories leading up to their severing there was a brief moment where I was connected to... someone."

"Jacob." Jack thought, but tried to keep his mind clear beyond that. If she could enter his mental construct, then he had to consider the possibility that she could also do much much more. If she could, she didn't let it show.

"While I couldn't tell much from the connection, I could glean a few memory fragments. One of those led me here. This is good, by the way." She said with a smile.

"Aye. I've long thought so." Jack had to admit, the woman was captivating. In other worlds he would have wanted to spend more time getting to know her. But here it just made him that much more suspicious. "So what is it you're after here, lass?"

Set downed the remainder of her beer and slammed it down. "Ever to the point, aren't you?" She said with a smile. "Fine. Your underling implied you have a way out. I want to see what I can do to speed it up."

"Easy. Give me your power. I'll probably be able to break us out with that."

"Come now, Jack. You can't just meet a girl and ask her to sign over her life on the first date."

"You claim you have the memories of me team mates. I dunno which of them you have rattling round up there but I do know this: every bloody one of the folks lost knew they could trust me. Search their thought, you'll see." Jack tried to tamp down his own expectations that he could talk her into this, but it was tough. He realized that if he could get her to sign over her power, he could finally be done with this whole mess. No more playing god. No more politics and lies. He could safely and finally end all of this. "You do this, lass, and you'll be free. I can break us out of here, I know I can. If I'm wrong, I'll give you back every last soul you loaned me. Hells, if I'm wrong I might even give you me own just to escape this nightmare. Search those memories, Lass. You can trust me."

Set looked torn for a moment, but as Jack feared, he quickly saw the look of iron take its place behind those eyes. He knew before she spoke that this would go nowhere. Never the less, he listened intently to the answer she gave.

"You are right. I have many years worth of memories telling me you are trustworthy. But I also have millennia of memories that tell me otherwise. I wish I could believe what you say, but the lessons I learned on that topic were too well taught."

"Somebody betrayed you." Jack had seen it before. It made much of what she did today more understandable but it made his options more limited.

"Yes. Long ago, but so thoroughly that I will never forget it."

"Who was he?" Jack hoped beyond hope that if he could help her to overcome her past, perhaps he could win her over. One moment of trust was all he needed. "Someone in your life or after your death?"

"After. As to who, it no longer matters. What matters is the lesson. I had power, as did he. He convinced me that if we pooled our power, we could over take those that were a danger to us."

Jack sighed, knowing where this story was headed. "That's when he betrayed you."

There was a moment of sadness visible in her eyes, replaced quickly by a red hot anger that took Jack aback. "Yes." She spat. "He took the power for himself and stripped me of my own will. My being. I was nothing, for at least a century. Nothing but a piece of power for him to wield at his leisure. If he'd not been stupid enough to get himself trapped in the Great Wall I might still be nothing."

She brought herself up to an impressive height and exuded power as she stared down at him. "So no, Jack. I will not ever make that mistake again. Not for you or anyone else. So I ask you again, is there anything else I can do?"

Jack sighed. "Stay out of me way."

"I thought as much. But know this: I have my own ideas, and now that I know someone else has found a way, I'll be redoubling my own efforts. "

Jack wasn't entirely certain if he should read that as a threat or not. He decided the smart thing was to play it polite. "Understandable, Lass. Good luck to both of us, then."

Set smirked. From the looks of it, he had caught her off guard. "Good luck, indeed, Jack."

And with that, she was gone. Jack scoured the entire construct, but could not find any sign of her. Still, he no longer felt completely safe. That thought disturbed him. "If you aren't bloody well safe in your own head, what do you have?"

He was only slightly relieved that nobody answered him.

Chapter 21

"**I**s everyone comfortable with their part of the plan?" Thomas worried about asking that question too much, but worried more that the team might not be prepared for what they were going to do. This was by far their most risky plan yet.

"Yo, don't worry, man." Shantae said with a wide smile. "We got this."

"Trust your team." Senebkay added.

Thomas did. The plan had been well thought out and was as sound as it could possibly be. Cho had contributed greatly to that with his recommendation that they mimic what Coughlin's group had done to him. Everything looked good, which is what scared Thomas. There had to be something he was missing. It could never be that easy. But, in the end, there was no denying the risk was worth it.

"Okay. Be careful. Leo? Are we ready?"

The Italian nodded, not taking his eyes from his pool. "The information you gave, Thomas, it was good. The path is ready to open."

Thomas nodded. He hadn't bothered to tell Leo that the information had come from the man's own memories. It didn't seem like it would have been helpful. He hated keeping secrets, but sometimes it no other path made sense. "For the greater good, right?" He thought without comfort. It concerned him how much Senebkay's point of view had started to make sense to him. "Okay. Shantae, Cho, you two are up. I'll be watching. If things go wrong, I'll yank you back and we'll make a stand here."

"We'll be fine, Friend Thomas." Cho said as he walked to the pool. He then turned to Shantae and Leo and nodded for confirmation before he stepped into the pool.

Thomas immediately smelled the sulfurous scent through his link. The memories of the battle where he had lost Jack and Charlotte hammered into his head, despite his best efforts to drive them out. This place existed as, not unexpectedly, a near exact replica of that dread battlefield. The seemingly burned wasteland that felt simultaneously both too uncomfortably cold and ridiculously hot, the stench that burned the nostrils, the obnoxious hum just at the edge of hearing. It was designed to be hell, and it lived up to that design. But for now, it was also desolate, which meant Leo had done his job in finding a corner. Thomas fought down the horrors of his memories and focused on doing his own job.

With Senebkay's instruction, he worked to mask Cho's presence, hiding it from anyone who might be looking. It might not have been possible without having joined Cho to himself, but one of the advantages of their setup was that he could pull much of Cho's power out and scatter it among their other teammates. This left it for Cho to draw off of in an emergency, but left his energy signature faint enough that it was unlikely to spark notice from anyone not specifically seeking him out. When he felt confident it worked, he gave the mental go ahead to Shantae.

"Time for me to do my thing, then." She smiled as she stepped into the pond herself.

Thomas felt the shift in his senses as she encountered the same destination. Again he worked to redistribute her energy so that it would be less visible.

"Okay, they're in." He whispered to Leo and Buster. "Be ready, we'll go in as soon as Shantae has done her part."

Buster nodded, since the last part was directed at him, and padded over to the pond without a word.

"Yo, this place SUCKS." Shantae replied in his head. She'd taken to their communication faster than the others. Thomas wasn't sure if it was a product of the shared memories or her natural adaptive nature.

"Yeah. I agree. Can you seize it?"

Shantae took a moment to reply, obviously digging through the unfamiliar architecture of the corner of Hell she'd found herself in. "Yeah. I think so. There's a choke point where it connects to the next sanctuary. I think I can tie that off so that no one on the other side notices immediately that this side's gone. That'll give us access to..... three Sanctuaries worth of souls I think?"

Three Sanctuaries. That was a lot of power for the Soul Stone if things went right, and a lot of potential power directed against them if things went wrong. But again, Thomas reminded himself, this is what they came here for.

"Do it. Let me know when you've got it."

The waiting seemed to take forever. Cho scouted the immediate area while Shantae continued working behind the scene to seize control. Since Thomas didn't want to risk messing with Shantae's concentration, he mainly focused on Cho's awareness. There was nothing visible anywhere within a mile of where they landed. That worked well for their plan, though Thomas knew it could quickly change if whatever controlled this place learned of their presence.

"Almost got it...." Shantae advised. It had been more than an hour after they had started, and thus far they'd remained under the radar. Thus far, all had gone according to plan.

Thomas thanked her for the update, and advised Cho to return back to the rendezvous.

"Leo, how's the path?"

"She is still stable, Thomas."

"Good. Buster?"

The dog nodded. Thomas knew he was ready. The dog was always ready.

"Got it!" Shantae screamed in his head with a laugh. "What a rush!"

"Don't get too cocky." Thomas cautioned her. "The hard part's just beginning."

"For you." Shantae correct him. "For me this is the less dangerous part."

To a point she was correct. Thomas didn't bother correcting her that if this next part failed and he and his companions went down, she would likely to be stuck in that hell of a sanctuary for eternity. No point in adding any more pressure. Instead he turned and nodded to Buster, then braced himself and stepped into the pool.

As bad as the realm was when experienced through the senses of his companions, actually being there felt infinitely worse. It reminded him of the time he had walked in four hours after his roommate had fallen asleep cooking some kind of cheese biscuits. The memory was far from pleasant. He wanted to dampen his senses, and especially those of Buster, but decided the risk of being caught off guard by the demons that inhabited this place far outweighed the extreme discomfort.

Instead he tried focusing his attention elsewhere. "What direction?"

"There" Shantae pointed. "I can sense some serious power concentrated that direction. I can start unraveling some of it, but not without notice. I'm pretty sure they have to be damn cocky not to have noticed us yet. I push any further and they'll have to be actively ignoring us to not know."

Thomas nodded. "I still feel like that's our best bet though. Cho? Buster? Get ready for incoming. I think we're about to have company." Thomas produced the Soul Stone and handed it to Shantae. Senebkay had assured him that she could do what they were planning to do with it, though he still wasn't entirely convinced. "Remember everyone. We don't have to beat them, we just have to keep them off of Shantae.

Buster crouched like a tightly wound spring. Cho gave a quick "Yes, Friend Thomas" then assumed one of his now familiar martial arts stances.

Shantae took the stone and nodded. "Just tell me when, Sugar."

Thomas didn't like this. It was a huge risk. But he reminded himself that his team was strong and they could do far more than he would ever have thought possible. And their options were limited at this point. "On my mark..." he sighed. "NOW!".

A strange wind brushed across Thomas's face. After so much stillness, he knew that it was unlikely to be coincidental, but aside from that it remained quiet.

"Maybe they won't notice?" Cho offered helpfully. Thomas wanted desperately to believe that, but it seemed far too optimistic. His pessimism proved warranted a moment later.

"There." Buster growled, nodding to the horizon.

Thomas looked, at first he saw nothing, then he realized that the sky was rapidly darkening. It took him a moment to realize that it wasn't clouds darkening the sky.

"That is a lot of bats." Thomas's heart sunk as he had a brief flashback to flying through the flock of birds guarding Leo's plateau. He would have vastly preferred to fight another demon than this oncoming swarm. One giant creature would have been far easier to keep busy than millions of small one. But there was no turning back now. They would never get this chance again if they ran, and their only chance of Coughlin not finding out required them to erase all traces of this sanctuary before he decided to look for it.

Thomas quickly looked back at Shantae. She was lost in her work, oblivious to the oncoming swarm. There was no way she'd be able to keep up her concentration in the middle of a mass of wings and fangs. "Okay." Thomas said to himself. "New plan."

He raised his arms and pictured a dome of energy encompassing him and his reader. He wanted to expand it out to his other friends too but knew the only way he could hold it that large would be to take their energy back into himself. That seemed more of a risk than leaving them on their own. For now....

"Shantae, any chance you have to speed things up will be appreciated."

"Not helping, sweetie."

The swarm blazed forward to less than a hundred feet away. There was no visibility any direction. There must have been millions of them. "This is going to suck."

The bats slammed into his shield with the force of a bulldozer. Thomas grunted despite himself, but managed to hold up. He reached out tentatively to his cohorts. Cho danced about in a blur of spins and punches, Buster became a whirlwind of fanged death. Both were dishing out far more damage than they were receiving, but the swarm was legion. For every ten that fell a hundred more seemed to hit. Thomas grunted again and had to pull his focus back to keeping the shield in place. He ran an electrical current through it, causing the hair on his neck and arms to raise up and charging the air with ozone. The result was positive as it caused fast growing pile of tiny mammalian bodies to begin piling up. Unfortunately, it also sped up the energy drain to a frighteningly noticeable level. After a moment he dropped that feature, focusing purely on keeping the field up and in place.

There were too many. The field around him continued to get pummeled from all direction. He risked a quick feel of Cho and Buster. Both were still holding their own, but to his horror both were noticeably slowing. This was a horrible plan. He should never have listened to Senebkay.

The last time they had challenged one of Coughlin's demons they had lost a whole team of experienced fighters. Why had he thought they would fair so differently this time?

"Because you have tools they didn't." It was Senebkay's voice, but didn't see the Egyptian anywhere about. "For all our sakes, USE THEM."

Thomas knew what Senebkay meant. Pull in his team, fight them with the exponential power that came with enslaving multiple souls. For a brief moment Thomas considered it, but doing so immediately brought the risk to mind.

Pulling his team might very well mean handing that power over completely to the Egyptian, and he was not ready to do that. "No. But there's another way. Sorry Leo."

Thomas reached out to the Italian. Just as he'd pulled energy from Shantae and Cho to hide them, he now pulled energy from the Italian to replenish his own. He felt the shield strengthen, felt the pummeling lessen. He reached out through his links and pushed some of that energy to Buster and Cho. Their speed returned and their attacks redoubled.

Leo was in his own Sanctuary, so his energy reserves were filling fast, however Thomas was pulling that energy out for three people. This bought time, but that was all it did. It was not going to work for long.

"Almost got it."

Thomas hazarded a glance over his shoulder to Shantae, who held the soul stone high above her head. It glowed with an expanding aura of blackness that was rapidly sucking in the light around it to the point that Thomas couldn't actually see the rock or even the reader's hands as she held it. "Good."

"Defense," he reminded himself as he fortified the shield. "We don't have to win. We just have to hold." They could do that. At least for a little longer.

Thomas inched backwards until he was just a little in front of Shantae, allowing the Shield to compress to a smaller size. Less room meant less tiny bodies slamming into it, which meant less energy expended. He could feel Leo's energy levels getting dangerously low. Thomas reviewed other options. He could still reach out and tap his parents for energy, but he really didn't want to involve them. They had never volunteered for this and Thomas worried that bringing them in, even in this capacity, might put a large bullseye on them that he hoped they might otherwise avoid. Still, it was better than losing his team and each moment weakened them noticeably more.

"There!" Shantae screamed, and slammed the rock into the ground. Thomas closed his eyes and braced himself for whatever was coming. He had no idea what to expect, but he knew something was about to happen.

That something turned out to be nothing. No sound, no bodies slamming against his force field, no screams from his companions. Just silence. Thomas cautiously opened his eyes and was surprised to find himself sitting on the Rainbow Road. He turned quickly and felt relief to see each of his companions still with him. Buster and Cho looked more drained than he had seen them in a long time. Shantae, however, was holding out the glowing black stone and grinning from ear to ear.

"Piece of cake!" She laughed. Thomas shook his head. He his exhaustion exceeded his ability to try and correct her, so he instead took the stone with an nod.

"Thank you. Let's go back to the plateau."

It took most of his remaining energy to gather his friends and quickly teleport them all back to Leo's sanctuary.

Had any of them been more rested, they might have spotted the Angelic figure that watched them leave.

Chapter 22

"**A**re you ready, mate?"

Darius shook his head. "Honestly, no but..." He looked off, pausing for long enough that Jack started to ask if the man was still with him before finally finishing. "It's not like there is much of a choice left, right?"

Jack shook his head, attempting to look as sympathetic as possible. "No. Not really."

Darius had requested a day on his own. He'd spent it under guard, of course, but it was a wish Jack had readily granted. After having Set suddenly turn up in the safe house within his own head, he was beginning to worry about the plan of tying these more experienced souls directly to himself.

Not, as Darius had just stated, did he have much choice left. Each alternatives risked turning all power over to Set, an unacceptable risk, leaving this as the only play he had.

"Alright then, mate. Let's get this over with. Promise I'll be gentle."

Darius looked at him in a moment of confusion, then shrugged his shoulders. "Perhaps this will grant me insight into these odd cultural comments of yours."

Jack laughed. "Not bloody likely. Me own mates don't get all my jokes and they were alive around the same century." With a now practiced motion, Jack reached into his shoulder and pulled out a silver cord. With a nod, he reached around Darius's shoulder and pushed the connection home.

The rush of power dropped him to his knees. Darius had one seventh of all of the souls that existed in the Greek realm. While he had experienced access to that power through the Helm, it paled compared to the intoxicating rush of having them directly linked. The desire for more and the disgust for what he was doing combined in a way that made him feel like a heroin junkie.

"Bloody hells. I never want to get used to this."

Darius nodded. "It is a burden and a blessing. You are now directly responsible for thousands of souls. Do not betray us."

With a rare complete bit of honesty, Jack replied, "I'll do my best by you, Darius. And the rest."

That best meant freeing them from this wretched realm. Anything beyond that mattered very little as far as Jack was concerned. "You're safe again, though. As promised, I'll do my best to stay out of your head and respect your privacy. Go in peace and all that."

Jack could feel the mix of nervousness and relief from Darius. He could tell from the man's surface thoughts that he had fully expected Jack to start immediately abusing the link between them. Jack noted with surprise that the man was far more suspicious than he ever let on. In this case, he probably had a right to be, but Jack didn't plan to do anything to the man if he could help it.

"Thank you, Jack Macintyre. I will."

Jack waited until the man moved completely out of earshot before turning to the other soul who had appeared in the room. "Goo'day Jacob. How goes the good fight?"

He didn't expect much of a response. Jacob had never been what one would consider talkative, but his time as an angel of death had turned his mood as black as the soul blade he wielded.

"You told me to check in with you if something weird happened. So I'm here."

Jack raised an eyebrow. "Sure, lad. What's up?"

"Two of your 'council' seem to be conducting their own investigation into the deaths."

Jack scanned Jacob's thoughts for the memories the members referenced. He saw them immediately, identifying the two men asking questions on the docks. "Argos and Telekos. Interesting."

"You said to cause a stir. It appears they've taken notice. It's what you wanted, right?"

"Aye." Jack shrugged. "But I'd hoped it would take them a wee bit longer before they started getting that curious."

As he thought about it, it didn't really surprise him. Telekos had an eye for details, and both men were prone to action rather than discussion.

"Don't look like they are too close." Jacob advised. "They're checking things out, asking folks that aren't connected directly to them some questions, but they're following up on some unrelated stuff from what I can tell."

That was good to hear, as far as Jack was concerned. While the helm could give him some basic information about the two, it by design couldn't read what the men were thinking. That meant Jacob's observations were likely to be the best he was going to get until they decided to bring him into the loop of whatever they thought they found.

"Slow down the reaping, but don't stop. Where possible, spread things out more and make it look as random as possible. I do need to keep them concerned, but Argos in particular is reckless. The bloody fool would probably charge Set herself if he got too worked up, and that wouldn't do any of us any good. Cept maybe Set."

Jacob nodded. "You're the boss." He turned to leave once more.

"We're close mate."

Jacob stopped. "What?"

"We're close. I know it doesn't seem like it, but I feel it. We're going to get home."

"Yeah." Jacob replied with a shake of his head.

Jack didn't need their link to know the man didn't believe him. He followed Jack's instruction because that was what he did. He might grumble about it, but Jacob always followed orders. Jack could tell that the man had already resigned himself to this new life. He was death, and death did not get an escape.

"I'll make this right." Jack whispered to himself as his companion disappeared. "Whatever it bloody takes, I will make this right."

Chapter 23

Thomas stared out from the top of his tower. He regretted that he did not get to spend near enough time here. The view provided a soothing comfort that he did not get near enough of these days, and the fast energy recovery felt absolutely delightful. After the draining experience of the hell-scape he had ordered each of his members to take time to recover at their sanctuaries. Impending apocalypse or not, they deserved that much.

He looked down at the soul stone in his palm. It pulsed with a blackness so dark it completely obscured his entire hand. He shuddered to think how many souls and soul fragments he had actually locked away in there, consigned to whatever oblivion the stone consisted of.

"They were all bad people."

Thomas looked up, and marked at how unsurprised he was these days when Senebkay just appeared and read his mind.

"I'm not reading your mind. It's my mind as well. We just share thoughts."

"Then why don't I ever read your private thoughts?"

"You don't have the practice I have of fragmenting your mind. You will. If you keep us alive long enough. And if you stop being so stupidly polite."

Thomas ignored the jab and focused on the stone. "So is this it? Do we have enough power to forge one of those weapons you were talking about?"

Senebkay nodded. "Yes. But I recommend that you don't."

Thomas looked up, confused for a moment. "What? I thought that was the whole point of this."

"It was." Senebkay spoke with the hint of irritation he always held when explaining something he felt obvious. "And if we were going on the offensive against Coughlin we still would, but that's not going to be your next move, is it?"

Thomas considered for a moment. "No. I think it's time we freed the Great Spirit. He's been trapped long enough. You object to that?"

"Doesn't matter if I do." Senebkay said as he walked over to the balcony and looked out over the horizon. For an instant, beautifully colored temples appeared over golden sand, before the untamed forest returned and replaced it. "Though in point of fact, it's not a bad play. Coughlin still holds more power than you do, and unlike you he's shown willingness to use it. You have me, but I'm not positive that is enough to tip the scales."

"Well, glad to see you've got so much confidence."

"I never trusted advisors who didn't give me straight information. You shouldn't either. Besides, there's a good chance that we can still earn a useful boon from this Medicine Man if we can bring him back. Which is why you don't want to forge a blade."

"So you've got a plan?"

"Don't I always?" Senebkay smiled. "This Great Spirit of yours and his souls have become wraiths. Soul blades are worthless against such things. Soul stones, however, are not."

Thomas felt from Senebkay's tone that the rest, should be obvious, but it wasn't. "Okay, so why?"

Senebkay sighed. "What did I tell you about wraiths?"

"They're souls cut off from their sanctuary, trapped in the Prime with no energy."

"More like negative energy. They're so drained that they need to collect energy to get back to zero. That's what makes them so dangerous. They usually need more energy than any one soul can provide, and that's for a normal wraith. A God Wraith might need more energy than even another god could provide. Luckily for us, he's scattered many of his souls out, so it should take significantly less energy than it would normally do to get him back to zero. That's all we need if you then link him back to one of your Sanctuaries."

"And the soul stone is a giant dose of energy."

"Enough. Hopefully. But there's a caveat."

Thomas shook his head. There always was. Senebkay's plans rarely came without risk. "And that is?"

"We have to get past the subordinate wraiths first. The stone doesn't have near enough energy to power them all, and if we use it on them first, it won't filter back fast enough to the source to wake him up. We'll have to save it for him."

Thomas considered what he was saying. "So what are our odds of getting past the other Wraiths?"

Senebkay turned serious. "That depends on many factors. If we only encounter one, you can probably expend enough energy to keep all of your team alive the way you like to do things. If we get too many more, you will be forced to bring your subordinate souls into yourself. You know I'm not lying to you on this."

Thomas turned away, realizing that all of his intuition told him the man was being fully truthful. He had avoided this option every time Senebkay pushed it so far, but he knew deep down that the moment might come when he couldn't avoid it.

"Soul energy multiplies when combined. If you go in with all of your souls withdrawn, you will be able to absorb more energy and you'll thereby be able to survive more wraiths. This is simply the way it works, Thomas. You can choose to avoid going in, but I do not want you to get us all destroyed because you choose to go in without being willing to do what needs to be done to survive."

Thomas's mind flashed back to the vision he had experienced of himself as Senebkay, bringing down the wall at the expense of everyone he loved. The horror of that memory chilled him every time he thought about it. He would fight to keep from losing control if at all possible, but that option kept coming up. "I will do what it takes to keep us alive." Thomas said flatly. "But I will not do anything to risk anyone I do not have to."

"Being a leader means making tough choices, Thomas. Whether you like it or not, you may reach the point where your only choice is which sacrifice hurts the least."

Thomas feared there was truth in the pharoh's words. More than he wanted to accept. "I think I'd like to be alone for a bit."

Senebkay stared at him for a moment, then disappeared. Thomas had no idea if the piece of his soul still floated about invisible or not, and for the moment didn't care. The darkness of his options consumed his thoughts, and for the moment, he allowed himself to wallow in the self pity that accompanied them.

Chapter 24

"There's more to this. I feel it." Argos growled.

"I do not doubt it." Telekos responded. "The questions are what and where."

"And who." Argos growled again. Telekos didn't respond to that. Argos knew the man well enough to know he bought in fully to the idea of Set being behind the attacks. Argos wanted to believe it too, but something since their investigation started seemed... off. One of his many memories of dying involved him rushing headlong into an attack against an enemy, only to be betrayed and murdered by one of his fellow soldiers who apparently had been jealous of him. He couldn't really remember if the event had actually been the end of one of his own lives, or the memory of some soul he had absorbed during the War After Death.

In the end, it mattered little. The lesson had been so painfully driven home in the last few seconds of that life that it could not be forgotten. When things seem too obvious, look deeper. Don't trust what you're told. Anyone could betray you.

But so far there had been little to really suggest anyone stood behind this. That was, of course, not possible. Souls didn't just disappear. Even those who went to the underworld could be traced along their route to the ferryman. The audit system had been argued to death in the early days by those who worried about one of their own slowly gaining too much power. While they were united in their opposition to Set and the other various opponents of the day, "enemy of my enemy" didn't create a good starting point for trust. He had to admit he had scoffed at the idea initially, but it had come in handy here.

"It's getting late." Telekos stated nonchalantly. "There's no point in pursuing this further tonight. Meet me at the east dock after sunrise and we'll follow up with the latest victim."

Argos merely nodded. Telekos stubbornly held onto the ideas of life such as time mattering and the need to treat lessor souls like they were living subjects with their own autonomy. It was annoying but predictable. Argos knew by now that no amount of pushing would keep Telekos going. That didn't mean that Argos planned to stop himself.

As his fellow god wondered back towards the citadel he called home, Argos turned back towards the docks. He wanted to inspect a loading zone used by the Priests of Set where an attack had occurred. It was the first such attack in ages, and as best as he could tell it had occurred around the same time that this mess had started. He'd visited it multiple times over the weeks since he had started this investigation and never found anything out of place but it still felt "off" to him somehow. He couldn't help but think that he still missed something crucial.

The air smelled a bit salty for his preference, but as a God that was easily fixed. The others often insisted on realism, but Argos always found that idea stupid. What was the point of building a world if it wasn't going to reflect your will? He had won the hard fought war. All should meet his vision of things. If the losers out there had some vague past life memory of things being different once that was their problem, not his. In fact, he should just...

"Hello Argos. It's been a while."

Argos paused. He knew the voice addressing him despite not having heard it directly in over a century. He spun around, his newly created short sword a hair's breath from the owner's larynx. She didn't so much as blink.

"How dare you break the truce. I should cut you down where you stand."

Set smiled and pointed down. Argos was forced to note that the woman stood just off the edge of the peer, a foot above the water. "See? I've not 'stepped foot' upon your lands. The truce remains in tact."

"A technicality". Argos growled. "Now tell me why I shouldn't take your souls now."

"The same reason you bluster rather than strike. You can't." Set smiled sweetly. Argos was about to test that theory when she continued with something that gave him genuine pause. "Besides, then you would never learn the truth about those actually betraying you."

Betrayal. He knew it. Argos pushed the sword slightly forward, to the point where a hair of blood would have trickled out of a real body. Still, Set did not flinch. "Spill your words, woman. Or I will see how many souls I can carve out of you before you flee."

"You know, don't you?" Set purred "You've figured it out already."

"I said SPILL YOUR WORDS."

"Your new leader. The God from behind the wall. He means to destroy us all."

Argos busted into a belly laugh. "Jack Macintyre? That is your boogeyman? The man is nought but a puppet. He has not the power to do anything. He holds no souls outside of those we lend him, and could just as easily take back. He is not the one you or I should fear."

"Does he not now hold the souls of Darius? I am told they now have a direct bond and it is not Jack who is subjugated."

Argos whipped his sword back into place. "And whose fault is that, wench?"

"Not mine. Come now, Argos, we fought directly for centuries. Do you honestly think I would cut loose such a prize then fail to seize it? Had I known how to pull off that separation I would have seized enough of you to tip the scales before the rest of you even knew it possible."

She had a point. Set had been the most ruthless of advisories during the Soul War. This would have been a sloppy move for her. Unless...

"How do I know you didn't do it just to see dissension in our ranks?"

"That might be a tactic Golnar would use, but not me. I have no reason too. If I wanted to take you on, I would do so, head on. As I am speaking with you directly today. Again, we have fought directly for millennia now. In that time have I ever lied to you?"

She hadn't. She was sneaky and conniving,ruthless to a fault, but so far as Argos could recall she had never actually lied to him or any of the others. Still, there was a first time for everything.

Set appeared to sense his distrust. "Fine. Let us do a soul share. I've no doubt you have a split soul in there somewhere that I can compliment."

Argos considered for a moment then nodded. He had not had the need of a Soul Share in centuries but it seemed appropriate here. He dismissed his short sword and reached back through his memories. It took him a few moments but he finally located a soul whose memories were missing, and who did not appear to have those memories with anyone connected to the Helm of Hades. He concentrated on that soul, and brought its essence into the palm of his hand.

"If the other half of this soul exists, it is with you."

Set nodded, then stared intently on the soul. After a moment a glowing ball of light appeared in her hand as well. "Ready?"

Argos stepped out then tossed the soul towards the ground between them. Set dropped hers in the same spot, and within a moment a Greek peasant stood between them. Argos suddenly remembered the man's rather dull history. How he had grown up in a small village, how he had taken over his father's sparse fields after the man died of infection, and how he regretted not being able to leave more to his two children as he lie dying of a similar disease. He would know if the man lied or even suspected the information Set sent him to be false.

"Did you have anything to do with the attack on Darius?"

"No." The man replied. Truthfully.

"Do you know who did?"

"I suspect Jack Macintyre, though I cannot prove it." Again, no falsehoods. Argos raised an eyebrow.

"Did you take the souls who have disappeared?"

"I have taken no souls on your lands." This was also true. Something seamed weird about the thought, as if perhaps there was more.

"Do you know who has?"

"No."

Argos furrowed his brow. "But you again suspect Jack Macintyre."

"Yes."

"Why?"

"I have seen within his mind. I know his end game."

"He says he can free us from this realm."

"Do you believe him?"

Argos hadn't considered it, really but now that he did, he knew the answer, and there was no point in trying to lie about it. Whatever he said would be perceived by Set as coming from the Soul, and she too would know its voracity. "No. The Glacier cannot be passed. If it could we would have found a way by now."

"And do you know what he plans to do when he fails?"

"Live out his existence until he grows too tired to continue. Then find a replacement like those of us before."

"No. I have seen his mind. He finds this entire life repulsive. If he realizes he cannot return, his plan is to unmake us all and consign every soul here to to the eternal sleep of oblivion."

This was a serious charge. And one that Argos had to admit made him feel feelings he had not remembered existing. Was this what fear had been like? He couldn't remember with certainty.

"Tell me you are certain about this."

Set waived her hand dismissively, and the split soul faded from existence, along with many of the memories it no doubt held. "You do not need to share a soul to know that I am. I would not bother being here, so near your shores, were I not. Contrary to what your people seem to think, I've no use for ruling all of this alone. The lack of worthy advisories would be... boring. But even that would be preferable to non-existence."

It made sense. He should have known better than to trust handing the Helm over to someone lacking the shared history the others had. It had seemed like a risk worth taking before, but now he knew how obvious of a mistake they had made. "Thank you. You are a worthy adversary. One willing to stand in the open on her own strength rather than pretend to be a friend while waiting to drop a knife in your back."

"What do you prepare to do, Argos?"

"Confront the bastard. Let him know that he cannot win with this. Let the others know of his betrayal."

"And what proof will you offer them? Your word? Mine? I assume there is a reason you are doing this investigation by yourself. Though you knew something was wrong, others would not believe you. What makes you think that will change now?"

"You have a point." Argos growled. "Damned fools spend too much time bickering and looking for hard evidence before acting appropriately. By the time they believe me it would be too late. Perhaps I should take him down myself. The others will not like it, but they will not oppose me once it is done."

"And if they catch you in the act? This Macintyre lacks the experience we have with wielding so many souls, but his plan is so intricate it even ensnared you for a time. What is to say that he may not have contingencies for just such an event that would lead to your enslavement?"

Argos turned and kicked a nearby crate of apples. It exploded in a cascade of wood and fruit. "I will not stand by while this upstart destroys us."

"Nor should you." Set replied calmly and deliberately. "But direct confrontation now would only play into his hands. Might I suggest doing something that he is unlikely to suspect?"

Argos attempted to fight down his anger. "What would that be?"

"Take your power. Disconnect from the Helm. Hear me out." She raised her finger before Argos could interrupt. "I have stated before that I have not lied to you. Nor shall I do so now. I will grant you safe passage past my lands to setup your own small kingdom. Between the two of us, we can shield it. They will not know where you have gone, but they will know I did not take you. This will cause them to start questioning each other, and re-evaluate what they think to be true. My spies will keep me updated on what is going on, and I will in turn keep you updated. Once they are ripe for the truth, you can return to lead them back to the balance that we have all managed to maintain these many years."

Argos considered, and nodded. "Yes. They would never suspect the two of us willingly working together. In the absence of true information, the suspicion will fall on the one who holds the Helm. And we both know that when that group decides to look for the full truth, as they no doubt will, there is nothing Jack Macintyre will be able to hide from them."

"I assume that you are... capable... of disconnecting yourself from the others?"

Argos raised an eyebrow. The wording sounded like a challenge. One that he could easily win. He closed his eyes and sought out his link to the helm. With a bit of targeted exertion he snapped the link in two.

The helm, and all of its connected souls, vanished. How strange it felt, he thought, not to be connected to the others. It felt almost like losing a limb. Still, it would be nice to strike out on his own for a change. Build a land as it should be built. In time he would, no doubt, come back to join the others, but only when they were willing to acknowledge the truth he knew and strip Macintyre of his power. Perhaps he would agree to become Hades again. Better to herd the cats than risk another mistake like this one. "It is done."

Set nodded, then gestured to the end of the peer where a large boat had materialized. "Then I will hold up my end of the bargain. Take this vessel and it will sail you to the edge of my realm. There you can create whatever kingdom you desire. I will lend my power to yours in keeping it hidden from the others."

Argos nodded. "I have been wrong about you. Perhaps when I return to being Hades, we should re-evaluate the relationship of our lands."

"Perhaps." Set smiled. "Though you would have to ensure that our relationship remained as interesting as it has over the centuries. But for now, go. Jack Macintyre will have already begun his search for you."

Without reply, Argos turned towards the ship, drawing in all of the souls linked to him in the process and using their energy to cloak his presence. He wished he could see Jack Macintyre's face as he became aware of the huge power drain he had just suffered. He sat and pictured the best scenarios in his head as the boat turned and drifted off into the haze of night.

Chapter 25

"It's so cold here." Shantae stated with a visible shiver. "And... dull..."

Thomas had forgotten that the newly dead woman had not been back to The Prime. "Concentrate on being warmer. You can't affect this world, but you can still affect yourself."

Shatae appeared successful in making herself comfortable, but still stared at her surroundings. "Is this really the... real world?"

"It is, friend Shantae." Cho added helpfully. "Or our view of it."

"Remind me when things slow down and I'll bring you back."

"If you survive." Senebkay added sarcastically.

Thomas ignored him and kept talking to Shantae. "You can even see some of the people that you left behind, though I recommend taking it slow with that. It can be a bit.... raw.... this soon after your death."

"Not sure I'm ready for that." Shantae replied. "But we'll see."

"This way." Buster stated, in his typical matter-of-fact voice. "Best if silent from here."

Thomas nodded and the team fell in behind the German Shepherd as he picked his way through the light forest. Thomas had no idea exactly where they had landed. He suspected the North Eastern US, maybe somewhere around Tennessee or Missouri , but in the end he could only guess. Buster had lead them through the Rainbow path to this place, and that was a trek Thomas had still not been able to stomach if he paid attention to it. He supposed it mattered little. Buster appeared to know exactly where he wanted to go, and as long as he remained their guide, they should be fine.

"Stop." The dog stated quietly but firmly.

The group did, and Thomas looked around. Silence covered the area. More so than he would have expected in the Prime. Even with its subdued noises, some variety of sounds normally came through. Not now. A thick blanket of silence covered all.

"We expecting trouble?" Shantae asked nervously. "Cause I feel like we're expecting trouble."

Thomas just nodded in a way that he hoped would satisfy and quiet her. He could feel the nervousness radiating from Buster, and that was something he was not used to. The dog didn't show it, but he obviously felt the worst afoot. Even more unusual, Senebkay seemed overly nervous as well.

Buster let out a low, instinctive growl but continued slowly forward. "He senses wraiths." Senebkay stated, a hint of genuine fear tinging his voice. "Lots of them. "

Thomas gave the man a dark look. He hated it when the Pharoah tapped into their friend's links without their permission, but he was somewhat afraid to chastise him out loud for fear of bringing unwanted attention.

"There's more of them than I suspected." Senebkay continued, ignoring or not noticing Thomas's look. "This is a bad idea. Let's get out of here."

Thomas shook his head no.

"Oh for gods' sakes, how many times do I have to tell you that I can hear your thoughts?"

"Sorry." Thomas thought sheepishly. He still hadn't gotten used to that. "But we can't turn back. Buster will get us through, and we have to make it to free the Great Spirit."

"You'll be of no help if you become a wraith yourself."

"RUN" Buster's tone brooked no question as the entire group took off after the dog, who bolted at top speed. The group zig zagged through the path, sometimes passing directly through obstacles while other times avoiding them all together.

Thomas caught glimpses of movement out of the corner of his eyes but nothing seemed to come into focus near them. In truth he couldn't be certain whether it was things moving in the real world or the wraiths they were all now afraid of.

The answer came when Buster slammed to a complete stop in a small clearing and began growling loudly and angrily.

"Trap." He hissed.

As if on queue, movement started appearing all around the clearing.

"Pull them all in." Senebkay demanded. "It's our best hope."

Thomas shook his head. There was enough power in the group to give Senebkay control of his body again. That chance scared him more currently than the wraiths.

Dark figures became visible, a mixture of what looked like rotted flesh and black smoke. The figures were all human like in shape, but bore little resemblance to their original forms beyond that. Brief flashes of their original humanity, a Mohawk here, dark long hair there, a few glimpses of actual eyes instead of blood red glowing dots, but for the most part it was hard to tell details about these things.

"I'm voting for the running now." Shantae stated, more than a bit of fear coming through her voice and connection.

"Agreed." Thomas gave in. He reached out to pull them all back to the training sanctuary.

Nothing happened.

"Pull them in." Senebkay ordered. "It's too late to run. We'll have to break through the circle and get away first, and it's going to be way easier with only one of us."

Break through the circle. Get away. That was a good plan.

"Buster. Get us out of here!"

The dog charged forward with a vicious bark. The rotting smoke creatures drifted closer, forming out of nowhere to close the remaining gaps between them. This was going to be close. Buster shot for one of the remaining openings...

And froze in place with a silent whimper. One of the smoke creatures erupted from the ground, grabbing hold of him. Buster fell.

"NO!" Thomas screamed in fear for his friend and a sudden freezing pain that erupted from the link he had to him.

"PULL THEM IN!" Senebkay screamed.

Thomas hesitated. Lose control to Senebkay or lose everything to the wraiths. That appeared to be his only options. One had a tiny chance of him regaining control, the other looked more and more like a fate far worse than anything he could imagine. He reached through the pain of Buster's link to pull the Dog into himself.

Again, nothing happened. Then, pain erupted through Cho and Shantae's links. Their screams created a cacauphany that shot fear through Thomas's very soul. "What have I done?"

"You idiot!" Senebkay growled. "When I gain control I'm never letting you out again. You're lucky I have a back up plan."

Thomas felt himself rapidly weakening, draining through the wraiths that were now burning his friends in dark acrid smoke. None approached him directly, but none appeared to need to. His energy rapidly depleted through their links. To his horror he could even feel his links to his parents and Leo starting to transfer energy through the open wounds that had been his friends' links.

"How do we shut them down?" He screamed to Senebkay.

"Do what I tell you when I tell you!" Senebkay growled.

Thomas nodded. There was no point arguing. Even his parents would be drained at this rate. Better he lose his own soul completely than that.

Senebkay closed his eyes and concentrated for a moment ,then snapped his fingers. In an instant, a set of massive roars erupted in the distance.

"What is that?"

"Something I hadn't expected to need this soon." Senebkay replied. "When I say pull, yank the souls in!"

Thomas reluctantly nodded. There seemed little choice now. Thomas looked around helplessly at each of his friends. They were completely buried now beneath the wraiths. Some of those had become more closer to rotting bodies than black smoke, their forms starting to become far more visible and defined. He wasn't sure if he was catching glimpses of his friends beneath those or if they had begun fading into black smoke themselves. He tightened a mental grip on each of the three links. Buster's grew faint at an alarming rate, which gave him a momentary cause of a panic. That panic turned to shock when... something... barreled into the clearing with another angry set of roars.

The beast looked to be a mass of creatures, shifting each piece with every step. One moment had elephant legs, a rhino head, bat wings and a lions body, the next moment a scorpion tale erupted with an aligator's head, an ostrich's body and spiked talons. It was a shifting nightmare but it crashed through the clearing and into the pile of smoke creatures on Buster.

"Pull!"

Thomas pulled and Buster's soul, weakened to the point of almost being gone, slammed into him. "What is that thing?"

"A Chimera." Senebkay snapped. "Get Ready!"

Thomas notices a faint silver chord going from the back of its shoulder. It wound softly through the air and attached itself firmly to... Senebkay.

"You! You were harvesting souls! Animal souls!"

The beast charged towards the pile that contained Cho, its form starting to slow its changes.

"You're damned lucky I was. Pull!"

Thomas yanked his Asian friend's soul in. It returned back with a crash of memories. Thomas fought them down and tried to focus on Senebkay. "You were gathering strength. You planned to take me over."

"I AM SAVING US! PULL!"

Thomas did so. A lifetime of confusion erupted in his mind as Shantae and Marcus's memories became his. A life of a woman trapped in a man's body. A life of shamed loves. The sadness of her only true love being ripped away by death. Thomas pushed them down as the world began to shift. They were leaving the Prime. His control began fading.

"NO! You can't have me!"

The world shifted. They were lost in time and space. No world, Prime or Sanctuary, existed around them.

"We've no time for this, Thomas. Let go."

Thomas pictured his friends. Their memories solidified as his memories. They were no longer in the forest, but they were still in the Prime. They were at his grave.

"Let go, Thomas. I will do what is necessary."

He saw the vision of the Glacier of Gods and Monsters crashing down, Titans crossing over it.

"I will do what you can't."

He saw his child scream. His wife cease to be.

"No!"

They shifted again. The room faded. He felt himself fading. He could barely make out a nursery. A light. A... woman's hand.... he reached out and took it. It was the only thing real.

"no" He whimpered. Warmth. The woman's hand provided warmth. Comfort. Power.

"No." She whispered.

Confusion. He felt confunsion. But it wasn't his, it was... Senebkay's?

"Impossible!" He heard the Pharoah exclaim. "How did you..."

Thomas cut off his voice. The man wasn't talking to him, but he didn't want to hear him anymore. He didn't have to hear him anymore. He knew that now. He knew all of Senebkay's secrets. There was so much the man had kept hidden.

"No." Thomas stated calmly. "No more."

Thomas opened his eyes. He was standing once more in the training sanctuary. Cho, Shantae, and Buster laid on the ground near him, slowly regaining their strength. Senebkay was no where to be seen.

Thomas smiled.

Chapter 26

"He bloody well had to have gone somewhere, didn't he?" Jack exclaimed.

"Indeed." Mikon replied in his typically unflappably tone. "And he shall be found. It is important that we remain calm."

"I'm with Jack on this." Golnar hissed, her velvety voice tinged with fire. "One of our own has disappeared for the first time in millennia. This cannot stand."

"When I left him he was still investigating the souls we suspect were taken by Set." Telekos added. "That can't be a coincidence. No doubt she took him too."

"No." Crisa stated, leaning forward in her chair. "A soul here or there, certainly. She could take those without us noticing. But tens of thousands? No, that kind of transgression would have immediately been visible to all of us. We would have felt her gaining that power."

"Well gods don't just disappear!" Telekos exclaimed.

Jack slammed both fists down on the table with a booming thunder that garnered everyone's attention. After a split second of looking around the table he stood and put his hands on either side of his head. "Okay folks, it's bloody well clear we don't know what happened, and arguing over conjector's not bringing him back. We're weaker against Set now, so we have to hurry against this in hopes that she doesn't figure out her advantage and try to use it before we find him. We've bloody well got nearly half the souls in this world at our disposal. Go. Use every trick you can to track him down."

The council members each nodded and then stood and filed out. Only Crisa remained. "I've not seen you this flustered since you took over the Helm. Even the attack on Darrius left you more calm."

"Aye." Jack nodded. "Well, you didn't arrive till after the fighting was over. And Darrius was still with us at that point. Argos isn't."

"Good point." Crisa nodded. "Still, have you detected anything out of the ordinary with him of late?"

"No." Jack shook his head. "I'd heard that he and Telekos had taken to investigating the disappearances on their own, but they hadn't come to me yet with any details and I hadn't seen any use in asking. I figured they would come to me when they found something. And unless you neglected to share a secret with me, this Helm doesn't allow me to read any of your minds."

"No. It doesn't. Okay, I have some ideas for following up on this. I'm sure you do too. I'll leave you to yours and I'll be off to mine. Good luck, Jack."

"Best of luck indeed, lass."

Jack waited till she was gone before he sat down in the throne and closed his eyes. He opened them and was immediately back in the tropical cabana within his mind. Huang, Heather, and Jacob each appeared moments later.

"Tell me you have some good news."

Each shook their head.

"No trace." Jacob responded, matter of factly. "I checked with all the souls connected to you. One remembered seeing him just after he left Telekos but he was till by himself then. Nothing out of the ordinary beyond that."

"I looked for any sign of the souls he took with him." Heather added. "No sign. It's like they all just ceased to be."

"He's just gone." Huang added sheepishly.

"Aye. Seems that way, but we all know that's impossible in this realm. He's somewhere. Either hiding by himself for some reason or being hidden by Set."

Heather walked over to a wooden table, shooed a fly away from the plate of fruit there, then grabbed a piece of pineapple and began eating it. "Why?" She said, after sucking some of the juice out of it. "Why would either do that?"

Jack shook his head. "I dunno lass. Maybe he figured out we were framing Set on the missing souls and got pissy over it? Maybe she took him out becauase he presented her with the opportunity but she was smart enough to somehow lock his souls away without taking them to throw us off? Too many variables. Hard to guess."

He looked over to Huang, who had an odd look on his face.

"What are you thinking, lad?"

The big man pointed at the plate of fruit. "I don't remember there ever being a fly in here."

Jack raised his eyebrow. There were always flies back in the origina cabana, but Huang was correct. That was not a detail he had ever thought to replicate here. He swatted at it, commanding it to be still as he did. It flew out the window on its own volition instead.

"Son of a bitch. Everybody out. Tell me when you find something."

Chapter 27

"Thomas!" Leo screamed with a level of concerned excitement that Thomas had ot heard from him before. "What happened, Thomas? Are you okay?"

"Fine." Thomas held up his hand, already starting to regain his strength. "Check the others though."

Buster was already standing, shaking his head. Cho and Shantae both remained unmoving, though Thomas could tell from their link that they were slowly recovering.

Thomas sat down on an already existing rock, still lacking the energy to create something more comfortable for himself. Buster padded up next to him and sat upon his haunches.

"Worse than expected."

"Yeah." Thomas replied. "Much."

Shantae finally sat up, holding her head as she did. "What the hells happened?" Her head suddenly dropped sideways in confusion. "And why do I suddenly know how to mummify a body?"

"The answer to both of those is Senebkay."

"That invisible dude you always talking to?"

Thomas nodded. "He double crossed me. Though I guess he probably saved us to, but that's beside the point. He'd been working on a way to take me over and seize control of all of you, and this gave him the chance he was looking for."

Cho finally regained enough energy to start standing. "Ugh." He managed softly. "Are you okay, Friend Thomas?"

"Yeah. I... I somehow managed to beat him back."

"Cause you a badass." Shantae smiled. "Pharoah's ghost underestimated you."

Thomas shook his head. "I don't think that's it. I think I ... must have had help. Master Ardru maybe?"

"This makes sense, Friend Thomas." Cho nodded. "He helped you last time."

"He did. But this felt different. I don't know. What I do know is that whatever happened gave me the strength to not only beat him back but actually see into his memories. Something I couldn't do before. I realized I couldn't get rid of him but I could sorta 'banish' him by splitting him between all of our minds. That still won't stop him if I have to bring all of you into me, but it'll slow him down for now and keep him from being able to take me over without each of you becoming part of me again."

"I guess that's a good thing." Shantae shrugged, obviously not completely understanding what Thomas meant. It was a reminder to Thomas that though she was an amazingly quick study, there was still a lot he needed to fill her in on. Not for the first time, he wished that he had some kind of manual listing everything it took to train someone like Jack trained him.

"It is. Though in the mean time I guess you'll have some unexpected knowledge."

"Yeah." She added with a shudder. "I could do without knowing how to pull some dude's brain through his nose."

"What about the mission, Friend Thomas? Do we try again or is it a lost cause?"

Buster perked up at this. Thomas was glad he could give them better news.

"We go back. But not the way we did before, that's obviously a bust."

"Well that's good news." Shantae added, wiping her brow. "Those dudes sucked. I do NOT look forward to fighting those bad boys again."

Thomas shook his head. "If all works out, you won't have to. When I looked into Senebkay's mind I saw that he had formulated another plan that he'd not mentioned. It seems dangerous, but he thought it would work. If he hadn't been trying to take me over, I suspect it would have been his first plan to go to. "

Thomas turned to his German Shepherd companion. "Buster, you'll be going in alone. Your stealth and familiarity will allow you to make faster time and have a higher chance of success than it would if all of us followed."

"I will do as you ask. Or I will die doing it."

"Let's try not to let the second happen. I'll be linked to you, and supercharging your energy. That's where the risky part comes in. I'll need to...."

"TOMMY!"

Thomas stopped and looked around. He immediately recognized his mother's voice as though she were right next to him. It took him a moment to realize that she wasn't.

"TOMMY! You need to get here! Now!"

"What is wrong, Friend Thomas?"

"I don't know, Cho, but I've got to go. Everybody get recharged as quickly as you can. I'll pull you if I need you!"

Without waiting for comment, Thomas instinctively reached out along the silver chord that linked him to his mother. As soon as he found the end of it, he willed himself to follow. The Training Sanctuary faded, giving way the the Prime. Between the chaos of movement and the dulled color and sound, it took a moment for him to realize where he was.

"My... my living room?"

Chairs were over turned. A group of uniformed individuals were huddled around something on the floor. Another stood over a wailing figure in the corner. His heart sank as the voice of the wailing figure came into sharp focus with a whimpered "My baby.... please..."

"Vitals are slowing!"

The reality of the situation hit him like a gut punch when his mother stepped over and grabbed him.

"Tommy!"

"What's happening? What's going on, Mom?"

She shook her head. The look in her eyes matched one of fear and horror that he had only seen once before from her... the day his father had passed. "I don't know Tommy. One moment everything was great and then.... She just went limp, Tommy. We don't yet know what's happening but...."

Thomas broke away from her and rushed to the huddled mass in the floor. The uniformed individuals were paramedics. He pushed through them, ignoring the vaguely weird sensation of going through their bodies, to get closer to his daughter in the middle.

"Charlotte! Charlotte, hang on baby. "

A second round of terror erupted from the corner where Shari was being held back at. "YOU HAVE TO SAVE MY BABY!"

"Miss we're going to take care of her. You've got to stay calm for us."

Thomas shook his head. "No baby. Stay with Mommy." It wasn't fair. He wanted to hold her more than anything in all the worlds, but not like this. Not yet. He wanted to be there when old age took her. He would wait for her after she had lived a long and healthy life. "Don't come to Daddy, Charlotte. Stay with Mommy. Please."

He reached down through the chaos and wrapped his hand around her tiny fist. For a brief moment, to his horror, it seemed like a tiny hand gripped his finger. "No baby. Not yet. Stay with Mommy, Charlotte. Stay with..."

An electrical shock ripped up his hand and into his body. His entire body briefly went rigid, then he felt energy poor from himself into the tiny hand. It was similar to what he had felt against the wraiths, though on a much smaller, far more sustainable scale. The feeling was accompanied by another, a sense of warmth. He recognized it immediately. It was the same feeling he had felt when....

"It was you." His eyes widened. "Ardru didn't save me, you did. But... how?"

A brief flash and suddenly his living room was gone and he was now standing in front of the Glacier of Gods and Monsters. Ahead he could see himself. "I remember this."

Wracked by pain, guilt and confusion after losing Jack and the rest, he had come here once. He watched the events unfold again anew. This time, however, he saw something he had failed to recognize before. A figure, trapped in the Glacier. A woman, dressed in robes that looked like they were probably early Greek or Roman in design. Olive branches and leaves were embroideried through out her clothes.

In a moment of fury, he saw his past self let loose a primal scream accompanied by one of the largest fireballs he had ever created. The fireball slammed dead center into the part of the Glacier where the woman stood trapped. After a brief flash and a loud crack, the woman was gone. A split second later, a portal opened over the river below and the fragments of the Glacier fell through it, disappearing from view.

He kneeled once again over his daughter, who now definitely gripped his finger in her tiny hand.

"She's stabilizing!"

A moment later she began crying. It was one of the most beautiful sounds Thomas had ever heard. Shari came crashing through paramedics, who leaned out of the way to let her pick the baby up. Thomas stood next to her, almost feeling as if the three of them were together, the family he could never have.

"Oh my baby." The sound of relief coming from Shari's near broken voice was palpable. "Oh you scared me so badly."

"We'll want to get her in for some tests, Miss. But she seems fine for now." A paramedic began explaining to her, as he was obiously trying to lead her to the door. "You can ride with us..."

Thomas tuned him out as his mother came up to hug him. "Thank god, Tommy. I was so scared for her."

"Yeah." Thomas nodded, still trying to wrap his mind around what had just happened. "I was too."

What had happened? What was his daughter? Had her stepping into save him caused her collapse? Thomas had way too many questions, but for the moment all he could feel was a sense of relief. Whatever or whomever Charlotte might be, she was most certainly his daughter. And for now she was safe. He renewed his resolve to ensure that she would always stay that way.

Chapter 28

"No! This is impossible!" Brother Parkes Coughlin struggled against the titanic figure that held him, but it was like struggling to escape a straight jacket. "You can't possibly be able to do this!"

Thomas Salazar smiled, his gigantic creepy maul looking as if it could swallow him whole. "Oh, but I am." His voice boomed like Goliath of old.

It made no sense. Salazar was a pup, a quick study with an old soul, to be sure, but he could not possibly have gathered this much power in that short of time. "No. It is impossible. How could you have..."

Thomas turned his gigantic body and held the helpless Coughlin aloft like a rag doll in one massive hand. The other pointed back. The old preacher could see it now. A silver cord, drifting in the ether. One end must have connected to Young Thomas the other....

"This can't be! I tried it! I connected to the Glacier and it almost destroyed me."

"You were unworthy. Your faith lacked. You quit where you should have pushed forward. Now... " Coughlin felt himself being raised up until he could see nothing beyond Thomas Salazar's massive eyeball. "Not you have failed. You have doomed your God. You have doomed humanity. Now all will serve ME."

"NOOOOO!"

"BROTHER COUGHLIN, ARE you alright?"

Parkes Coughlin glanced around. Miss Beatrice looked down at him with a look of deep concern. It took a moment to realize that he was sitting in the pews of Brother Giovanni's sanctuary. It was merely a vision. It hadn't been real.

"I'm fine, Sister. I just..." But it was real. Far more real than any vision he had ever had before. "Is Brother Giovanni about?"

"Of course," Miss Beatrice nodded, her concern only slightly faded. "I'll fetch him for you."

"Thank you." Coughlin replayed the vision in his mind. He had been having more of them of late, and fewer of them showed him achieving the goals he desperately felt he needed to do, but this... this was the first time he had finished one where he felt such abject certainty of his defeat. Something was wrong. Something had changed.

"Ahh, Brother Coughlin. I understand you have had a vision?"

"A terrible one. I fear... I fear we may soon be defeated if we do not do something drastic."

"Really?" Brighter Giavonni's angelic face took on its own level of concern. "Please, tell me what you saw."

Coughlin did, in great detail . He shivered involuntarily as he relived how powerless he had felt, how real it had seemed.

"So now you believe Young Salazar will harness the power of the Glacier?"

"I do. I do not know how, but that part seemed too real. It will happen and it will happen soon, I'm sure of it."

"Interesting." Giovanni stated as he sat back, no longer appearing as concerned as Coughlin thought he should be. "But hardly relevant to our task at hand."

"Hardly Relevant?" Coughlin felt incredulous. The Saint had always been a trustworthy advisor, but this... this seemed like an extremely naive statement. "If Young Thomas managed to harness The Glacier he could wield the power second only to our Creator himself. He could rewrite reality. He could destroy us in the blink of an eye."

"If.,.." Giovanni spoke as if he were explaining something to a child. "If Young Salazar connects to the Glacier, it will be for only a short time, and it will consume him. He would be lighting a campfire with the sun itself. You, above all others, know what it is like to try and wield that level of power. Do you think this soul, so newly dead, can do what you could not?"

"It seems unlikely but the vision..."

"Is just that. A vision. You know by now that visions can give us guidance, but they should never be taken literally. I myself have had many of late, and if they have told me anything it is that we are on the right track. We are, in fact, closer than we have ever been. Let your vision steel your efforts to do that which must be done with earnest and haste. A haste that you should put to use right now."

Coughlin tried to fight through his confusion. Giovanni had never steered him wrong in the near century that they had been together. Still, something about this seemed off. Giovanni might dismiss it, but he knew what he had seen. Yet, he could not dismiss the other's words completely.

"What is it you would have me do?"

"The reason I had sent Sister Beatrice to find you originally was that we have found another soul in need of your talents. I would have you go save them from the torment they suffer through, then avenge them with all of the fury of Heaven at your back."

"Very well." Coughlin sighed. "I will do as you ask."

"Excellent!" Giovanni exclaimed with a warm smile. "This scroll contains the details. God speed, my friend!"

Coughlin took the scroll and soaked in its information. A murderer and would be bank robber, his victims died painfully, bleeding from wounds that should not have been fatal had they been treated in time. He was gunned down himself before he faced justice for what he did.

Giovanni was right. He did have a job to do. Justice would need to be served to this man. But it could wait a short time. There was something he had to check for himself first.

Chapeter 29

"You summoned me?" Crisa asked as she entered the throne room. Her voice was even, but Jack got the distinct feeling that she was annoyed at being pulled back. He really wished he had the same information from his connection with her that he had from those directly tied to him. While claiming souls still left a bad taste in his mouth, he had to admit that knowing exactly what was on someone's mind made it far easier to deal with them.

"Yes. I'm sorry I pulled you away from the search for Argos, but... I've got a wee issue and frankly you seem to be the most likely to know what to do about it."

"Fine." Crisa stated non-chalantly, then took a seat at the large council table. "Sit and tell me about it."

Jack had to chuckle to himself. It had been at least a year or more since power had transferred from Crisa to him, yet she still often conducted herself as if she were in charge. He supposed old habits died hard. It mattered little to him, so he took a seat.

"Have ye ever created your own.... private getaway? In your head? Someplace you could retreat to when you didn't want to be disturbed."

"Yes." Crisa nodded. "Such places are commonly created among us. There's little in the way of privacy in the realm. Our own minds often provide the solitude that the greater realm lacks. Why do you ask?"

"Is there..." He hesitated, trying to figure out how best to ask her. It concerned him that he knew so little of what could happen here. "Is there any way that others could sneak into that world? Unbidden and uninvited by you the maker?"

"No." Crisa shrugged. "Not anymore. There used to be, but it should be impossible now."

"Are ye sure? You say you once could, how do you know it can't be done now?"

"Well because...." Crisa stopped, her eyes narrowing in a way that gave Jack some concern. Then her normal blank calm took back over, masking any thoughts she might have behind it. "Why don't you tell me what has happened. If I know more details I'll be better able to assist you."

Jack sat back in his chair, taking an instinctive deep breath. There was something here, something that had triggered a warning with Crisa. If he said the wrong thing, it might tip her off to some of the plans and mechanations that he had been working with behind the council's back this past year. That.... could prove very hazardous, especially with Argos's recent disappearance. He decided to skip the part about Set coming directly to visit and go for the most recent occurrence.

"So I have this little island cabana I've created in me head. Nothing fancy, based primarily on a place I loved to stay in life. As I said, I like to go there when I just want to get away and hear meself think. But this last time I noticed... well I noticed a fly. Quite normal for something that would have been there back in the real world but... well, not something I remember putting there on me own."

"So you suspect someone else put this bug in your hideout?"

"Is it possible? I mean, if it's just something that might have grown organically as a result of something over here that's one thing, but if someone's spying on me, well, I'd bloody well like to know about it, as you can imagine."

Crisa sat stiffly, her face a blank slate. It appeared as though she were contemplating numerous pieces of data, determining what was relevant and what wasn't. Finally she spoke.

"Anything created in your mind should come from you. It would be unlikely to spontaneously appear, though of course if your concentration laxed it is possible for your subconscious to create something your conscious doesn't intend to."

"And you think this is what happened, do you lass?"

Crisa shrugged. "I do not have enough information to make that guess. It is a possibility. And it should be the only viable answer."

"But I can tell by your tone you don't think it is the correct one."

Crisa raised an eyebrow. "We're centuries removed from the other alternative. However, many odd things have happened since you took on the Helm of Hades, so it is difficult for me to dismiss the alternative out of hand."

Many weird things indeed. If she knew half of what he had done without the council's approval, he suspected she would lead the mutiny against him herself. Still, there was a chance he could turn any suspicion to others, perhaps Argos given his strange disappearance. To do that he would need to know more, however.

"Aye, so what is this other alternative then?"

"Long ago, during the War of Souls, powerful Greater Spirits would occasionally allow small fragments of their true soul to be captured by others. This was a risky move, because if one lost too much of their true soul they could lose themselves with it, but doing so allowed... how to explain this.... a window to be opened into the mind of the one who captured the fragment."

"So is there a chance there's some fragment of Set's floating around in a soul linked to one of us? Darius maybe? "

"Set? No. Part of the peace accord was to ensure that she was in full possession of her entire soul, and each of us had possession of all of ours. I suppose it's certainly possible for Darius to be spying on you, since you now possess his entire soul, but it would be a great risk for him to do so. After all, you can scan his entire mind to determine anything he's done. Argos could also have done so before disappearing, though subtle subterfuge such as this would be entirely out of his character."

The docks. The priest that Jacob had captured in order to frame Set for the attack. All of the unusual occurrences had happened after that time. Bloody bitch had been one step ahead of him all along. Jack shook his head. This could prove very dangerous. Still, no use causing concern among the Council.

"Probably Darius then. I'll summon him and question him. As you say, I'll know if he's lying."

"Jack, I must ask: Have you reaped any souls directly from Set?"

Yes. "No, of course not."

"You're certain? Because if you did we'll need to....."

"Jack?"

It had been more than a year, but Jack recognized that voice without hesitation. "Thomas? How?"

Crisa's eyes narrowed. "Who is Thomas?"

"Jack! Follow my voice!"

Jack stood up, fighting to keep his ecstatic excitement as hidden as possible. He had no doubts that he was failing miserably, but he really didn't care that much. "Crisa, something just came up! I have to go."

He ignored her protests and teleported out of the room without notice, doing his best to follow the sound of the voice.

"I'm coming Thomas, you magnificent lad you! For gods's sakes, please hold!"

Chapter 30

"Dude!" Shantae exclaimed with glee. "This is.... this is off the charts, man."

Thomas nodded as they walked down the beach opposite the Glacier of Gods and Monsters. He had been here multiple times now, and it never ceased to fill him with wonder. The massive mountains of frozen River radiated power beyond anything he could even fathom. If he stared long enough, he could make out figures locked deep within the ice.

"These are the Greater Spirits of old. The gods that once walked the earth. Now..." Now they slowly melt away. He vaguely remembered what it was like for Senebkay to be locked within. Eons upon eons of being trapped, unable to do anything but slowly waste away. That had changed when someone... Brother Coughlin, had stupidly tried to control the Glacier. The attempt blew up a chunk of the Glacier large enough for Senebkay to escape.

Now that he thought about it, Thomas realized he had essentially done the same thing for whomever now lived within his daughter. That was a bit of a disturbing thought, the idea that she would have to deal with her own alternate personality the same way he's had to deal with Senebkay. Still, that was something for another day.

Today he had to concentrate on doing something incredibly foolish and stupid. Stupid, however, was sometimes necessary to accomplish goals. If Senebkay's calculations were correct, this would do exactly what they needed to free The Great Spirit.

"Buster, are you ready?"

"Ready" Came a thought in his mind. The link he had to the dog told him the same. The German Shepherd was already on the Prime, waiting for the signal to start his assault.

"Good. I'm going to try and establish as small a link as possible. I'll feed the energy straight to you. Use it as you need it, there's going to be more than enough. Cho? Shantae?"

Both figures next to him nodded.

"I may have to send excess energy your way. If I do, get rid of it as quickly as possible. Create something, attack the ground, do anything you want just DON'T attack the Glacier. Trust me, that can have... unforeseen consequences."

"We will do as you ask, Friend Thomas."

"He's got that right." Shantae added, visibly excited.

Thomas turned back and stared at the Glacier. He remembered quite clearly watching Coughlin attach himself. He wondered how many eyes stared at him now, waiting for the moment to be free from their centuries of torment. Thomas was going to do his best to make sure that didn't happen.

He did not intend to repeat Coughlin's mistakes. Coughlin wanted to control the Glacier, to take its power into himself. Thomas wanted to direct it, act as a conduit for a very small part of it as it passed through him and into Buster. With any luck, Buster would be able to use it to save the Great Spirit.

"Okay." Thomas said, trying to push down the nervousness balling up in what used to be his stomach. "Here goes everything."

He reached into his shoulder and pulled out a silver cord. He was careful to will it to be smaller than he would normally make it. He then held it aloft, and like a snake charmer willed it to slither into the air. It slowly drifted its way over the roiling River that pooled in front of the mountains of ice. He paused as it reached the edge of the closest Glacier, then before he could lose his nerve, surged it forward.

The rush of power dropped him to his knees.

"Friend Thomas!"

"I'm okay Cho. I... just..." He let the energy pass through him, a torrent of power that refused to be contained. He limited it as best he could, splitting small tributaries off to Cho and Shantae. The rest he aimed straight to Buster.

He could feel the loyal warrior's body electrify with power, and suddenly he shot off like a literal bolt of lightening.

Thomas tried to follow his progress, but something else caught too much of his attention. A link he had not felt in too long. With elation he followed it.

Thomas's surroundings shifted and he suddenly found himself in a room that appeared to be made within the Glacier. He was careful not to touch surroundings, floating just above the floor. A sliver cord drove into the wall. He could feel a very familiar life force connected to the other end.

"Jack!"

The response came back, faster than he could have hoped. "Thomas? How?"

Thomas could have cried with joy. He knew he had missed his mentor, but hearing his voice once again brought out emotions he didn't even realize were there.

"Jack! Follow my voice!"

There was a momentary pause, just enough to give Thomas a sense of worry he may have lost the link, but then just as quickly a new response came.

"I'm coming Thomas, you magnificent lad you! For gods's sakes, please hold!"

Thomas did. He had no intention of losing this chance to see his mentor. He didn't have to wait long, as suddenly Jack came flying through the link and into the room.

"Don't touch the floor!"

Whether heeding his warning or instinctively knowing on his own, Jack obliged, floating just above the floor as Thomas did.

"Thomas, Lad, how the hell did you do this? We're in the bloody Glacier aren't we?"

Thomas gave him a hug inspite of himself, one his old mentor didn't fight, and in fact seemed to give back in equal enthusiasm. Finally, Thomas pulled back.

"It's a long story. And honestly an accident. We're trying to wake The Great Spirit, and, well, linking to the Glacier became the best plan to do it. Once I was connected.... well that's when I could feel your link."

"Bloody hell, boy. That's a dangerous move. But I'm glad you've done it. I'm glad to see you overcame the Demon. Bloody impressive, lad. Bloody impressive indeed."

The demon. That fight had been an eternity ago in Thomas's mind. He had forgotten just how much had happened since then.

"Yeah, well, we did take it down but not without a cost. In the end it was Charlotte that did it. I'm afraid it... it cost her too much, Jack. She took it out but didn't make it much beyond that."

Thomas noticed a few tears curve their way down Jack's cheeks. "Gods be damned. Always like her to be the hero. Damned fool. How bout the others? Cho? Buster? Leo?"

"All good. We even have a new recruit helping us out. Still carrying on the good fight while you're away. How about the ones that disappeared with you?"

"Still with me. Trapped on the other side of the Glacier."

Thomas studied the room, then studied the links. He reached again into Senebkay's memories (the man had chastised him to use all available resources on more than one occasion). A plan quickly formed. "Look, I can't make guarantees, but I think I can turn the energy I'm draining back on itself and feed it through our mutual links. If I did that at high enough levels.... I think I could probably blow a massive hole through the center of this glacier along the path of your link. Big enough for y'all to escape through."

It would no doubt lead to some of those trapped in the Glacier escaping as well, but that was a chance Thomas was willing to take. They could deal with them down the line. For now, getting Jack back was his new top priority.

"Lad, you don't know how ecstatic that makes me. But we may want to hold off just a wee bit."

Thomas was surprised. He figured Jack would want to return as quickly as possible. "What, do you have your own paradise on that side of the Glacier?"

Jack let loose a great belly laugh. "No laddie. Far from it. We have bloody gods on this side of the glacier. The likes of which could make Coughlin look like a minor annoyance by the time it's all said and done if we don't handle it properly."

Gods . Of course. Thomas was beginning to hate the entire concept of Greater Souls. "Fine. We'll figure out a way. Now we at least know we can..."

Thomas's sentence was cut short as he felt himself yanked backwards into the wall. The acidic coating ripped a scream from his gullet as he fed energy into it to keep himself from disinigrating.

"Thomas! Lad! What the hell?"

"I don't know, Jack, it's like.."

Another yank sent him flying, this time he was able to stop himself just before going headfirst into the wall.

"I've got to go, Jack! I'll be in touch soon!"

Without waiting to see the man's response, Thomas flew back towards his body.

Chapter 31

Buster stood quietly at the edge of the forest of the Great Bear. There were no signs of movement, but his keen nose told him that the wraiths they had faced during their last attempt were not far. Now that he knew the scent, death was on the wind from all directions.

He did not know what to expect from Thomas's plan. There was much that could go wrong, and after his last battle he had little doubt that he might join the wraiths here in the forest before the sun rose once more.

If that happened, then it happened. He had given the Great Spirit his soul many seasons past. He had expected at the time that he would live or die by the Great Spirit's fate. He appreciated the faith placed in him in guarding Thomas and his family, but it still felt wrong that he walked freely while the warriors who stayed behind in the Great Spirit's care were cursed to this half existence. He would save his brothers and sisters or he would join them. He accepted either fate.

"Buster, are you ready?" Thomas's voice echoed in his mind.

"Ready" There was no turning back. He bristled his fur and prepared for the charge.

"Good. I'm going to try and establish as small a link as possible. I'll feed the energy straight to you. Use it as you need it, there's going to be more than enough."

Buster hoped so. He did not wish to abandon Thomas's cause here. But it was Thomas's cause. His cause remained that of the Great Spirit. Thomas had grown strong enough to walk his own path if the worst happened. He was a fine brave, and would make a fine chief if he allowed himself.

Suddenly the world changed. Energy coursed through Buster's entire being, so much so that he felt he might explode in the fury of the deep summer sun. Brief flashes of memories came unbidden, days past when he first gave himself to Falling Dusk and his cause. The Great Spirit had wielded power like this. Buster would now use it to free him.

Buster charged forward, seeking out the strongest smell of death. He would need to discharge this energy quickly to avoid being consumed by it. It did not take long for that need to happen. If the power of just him and his party had been a beacon to the the wraiths before, the power coursing through his veins now must have been like the morning sun. Shambling masses of smoke and death came pouring out of the forest towards him. Buster met them head on.

They moved quickly before. They very nearly stood still now. Buster became a whirlwind of power, bouncing from one to the other. His attacks were effective but strange. Every bite he took, every rake of the claws he made, produced more flesh. Smoke rapidly burned way, and a natural semblance of form took its place.

Buster was elated, but he knew it was too soon to take any semblance of victory. He could see braves fall off to the side, looking confused at their surroundings. Many of them were immediately set upon by the countless black forms shambling in from all directions. There seemed no end to these wraiths. They were as the spring crickets, in all places for as far as the eye could see.

"This takes too long." Buster did not know how long Thomas would be able to keep up this connection, and every one of his brothers and sisters he brought back immediately suffered their previous fate all over again. This was not going to succeed. He must go after the source.

Buster shifted directions and ran, still attacking anything that came within range of his teeth. A wall was building around him of souls slowly turning back to normal but then being consumed all over again. His path grew trickier to navigate. Buster decided to switch tactics, changing forms to that of a tiny field mouse.

The switch must have caught the spirits off guard, as his new form allowed him to easily dodge and weave through their masses before they could react. Within moments, Buster broke through their ranks and found himself on the other side of the horde. He turned back to his more fleet of foot dog body and bolted as fast as his energiezed legs could carry him. The speed combined with the sacrifice of those he had turned back and left behind to draw the horde's attention must have worked. The sounds of the wraiths fell away, and a few quick glimpses over his shoulder revealed that no pursuers had managed to keep pace.

Buster took stock of his surroundings and altered course to a place he had not been in some time. The Great Bear's Cave. The path remained easy to mark, as a great and growing sense of darkness loomed in the distance ahead of him, and every step he took towards it lowered the temperature by a noticeable amount.

By the time he stood outside, where he had spoken to the Great Spirit many times in the past, the surrounding temperature was so cold that he knew any breath he might have once had would have formed a chilled frost at each exhale.

Buster thanked the Great Spirit for the excess energy coming from Thomas. Even with its extra power, he felt himself slowing closer to his normal speed and power. He had no doubt that the group would never have been able to pass this threshold on their original plan.

The darkness grew more tangible as he lowered his head and proceeded into the cave. Even with the power he possessed now and the practice he had had in adjusting his vision since death, he could make out little more than rough shapes in the passage. Just enough to keep him on the path and not going through the walls. The path slowed his progress dramatically, and for awhile he feared that the horde of wraiths might catch up with him. But his fears appeared unfounded. The wraith were either unwilling or unable to pursue him this close to their master.

His master.

Buster had trouble reconciling the Great Spirit and the Great Bear being one in the same. This death and darkness that he felt growing with every step, the suffering of his tribe in death, these were a stark contrast to the man he had given his soul to. It felt like only months since he had last heard from the Great Spirit, but he realized that if what Falling Sparrow had said was true then it had been centuries since the old Medicine Man had actually been capable of talking to him.

This fate that he had only recently become aware of had befallen his soul family during the battle with the God Monk. This had been the price paid for victory. Buster felt that he should have some level of shame for not doing something sooner. He also, however, knew such thoughts were pointless. The Great Spirit had gone to great lengths to hide this fate from him. He had no way of knowing before, and perhaps that was for the best. He would certainly have failed at any prior attempt. Now...

A giant chamber forced Buster to stop his musings. He was close. He could sense dark, dread energy emanating from very near by, a cold nigh unbearable even with the extra energy still pouring in from Thomas. He stopped and peered through the darkness, focusing as hard as he could for the source.

There, in the corner, he could see it. A massive form shaped like a great grizzly composed of smoke and rotting flesh. It did not move, did not breath, did not seem aware, but Buster knew that it was the most dangerous thing he had ever personally been in the presence of. He could sense its hunger, the hatred it bore for all things like him that had energy the Great Bear no longer possessed. He did not know why it seemed to be hibernating, perhaps its great dark power was too much for even itself to sustain. Perhaps it was something the Great Spirit had managed to accomplish before finally losing control.

It mattered not. This was what Buster had come for. This was why he had spent all of those centuries in slumber before being reborn as a pup to be given to the Salazar family. This is what he had guarded Thomas for.

Buster knew there was no good plan to accomplish this, so he did the best he could. He attacked.

With a rush of speed, Buster lunged forward, grasping the throat of the Great Bear firmly and biting down with all of the force his River charged jaws could muster.

It was like holding a torch to a glacier.

A roar erupted from deep within the body of the Great Bear, suddenly energized by the very energy Buster pumped into it. The monsterous form rose up on its back legs, taking Buster up to a height at least four times his body length. Buster kept hold with his powerful jaws, pushing the energy coming in from Thomas through his teeth and into The Great Bear as fast as he could.

A gigantic paw caught him off guard, sending him flying across the room and nearly through the far wall. Buster felt certain that without Thomas' energy, that hit would have disapated him on the spot. With Thomas's energy, it merely slowed him temporarily before he bounced back to his feet and charged again. The Great Bear stood up now, angry and bellowing. It was too dark for Buster to really be able to take full stock on whether his attack had had any actual affect, but he knew he would have to continue.

Buster ducked another powerful swipe and slid beneath the giant creature. Once on the other side he sprung for the creature's back, again sinking his teeth in, this time near the scruff of the neck. Again he felt freezing blackness beneath his jaws, eagerly soaking in all of the energy he could pour into it. Still, the Great Bear fought. It was not enough that it consume energy, it appeared to have an instinctive need to destroy as well.

Massive claws reached back and raked Buster's sides, painful and deep, but there was less force in them from this position, and while they felt like frozen daggers raking his sides, they were not enough to break his grasp. Buster shut out the pain and focused on the one thing he knew for certain would make a difference: transferring more energy to the Great Bear.

The room seemed to be growing ever so slightly warmer. Buster wasn't certain if that was true or not, but he took it as a sign that he was succeeding. The Bear raked him once more, painfully ripping his sides again, but Buster continued ignoring it. It stood again and flailed, but Buster would not let go. Then, it did something Buster had not expected.

The Great Bear's form shifted slightly and suddenly Buster found he was again hanging from the front of the creature's neck. From this angle the giant beast easily lifted Buster's body up and once again delivered a stone shattering blow that sent the dog flying out of the room. Buster shook himself, taking just enough time to refill his own depleted energy before charging back forward. His was halfway back across the room when his momentum froze.

Everything else froze as well. Buster felt his energy levels begin draining from all around. With horror he realized that the torrent of energy coming through Thomas's link had shut down to a trickle.

"No! No! No!"

He was close, he could feel it. Even without Thomas's extra energy he was able to survive the room, and that was something he was certain he would not have been able to have done before. With his limited site, it seemed the Great Bear mostly appeared flesh and bone, now with only tinges of smoke and very little rot. But that made it even more dangerous. Now it moved with purpose, and its gaze fixed on Buster with cold determination.

Buster looked around, trying to keep the Bear circling. He could make his way back for the exit, but there were good odds that the wraith awaited him out there. He tried quickly to teleport but could feel his ability to do so being locked down. Whatever sphere of influence the Great Bear had on this area, it dramatically limited his ability to flee.

There was also the matter of whether he truly wanted to flee. Full of power, he had been certain that he would willingly give his soul to rejoin his tribe if he failed. Now, back to his normal levels of energy and draining, he was less certain.

The look in the Great Bear's eyes told him that final choice might not be his anyway.

"Fine." Buster stated, shifting forms once again to that of his human form, Running Wolf. "If I am to die, let it be as a warrior. I will rejoin my people if I must, but I will not go easily."

Chapter 32

"Thomas!"

Jack suddenly, inexplicably, found himself back in the throne room, his link to Thomas as distant as it had been since he woke up on this side of the Glacier.

"Ah lad."

The coldness of this realm settled upon him with a weight he had not realized existed before. Escape had always been his goal, and he had been aware that it was something that should be possible. He had also known it would be disgustingly irresponsible to do so until Set was taken care of. Bringing a god of that power back to the Prime was asking for a return to the days before the Glacier, and that was something he could not be responsible for.

Or so he thought. Now that the promise of escape was being dangled in front of him, he was less certain he had the resolve to not take it. He had told Thomas they needed to delay, but that was when he thought he would be able to blow the wall whenever he wished. Now, in this moment, cut back off from Thomas, perhaps indefinitely, he realized that might be a mistake.

Whether it was selfish or not was a tough call, but deep down he knew that he would not be able to re-adjust to life on this side of the Glacier. He had tasted a moment of freedom, had been reminded what existence outside this dreary cage could be like, and he could not stand the thought of it being his eternal prison.

"What did you do, Jack?"

Jack opened his eyes to realize for the first time that he was not alone in the the throne room. The voice had belonged to Crisa, whom he remembered had been speaking to him prior to Thomas pulling him into the Glacier. But she was no longer alone, either. The entire council, excluding the still missing Argos, stood around him. Even Darius stood in the group with an odd mix of fear and disapproval emanating from his link.

"Did I miss a call for a meeting?"

"You've been playing us, haven't you?"

Jack raised an eyebrow, quickly feigning ignorance. He obviously had been, but now wasn't the time to go admitting it. Especially when he had no idea how much or little they might really know.

"What are you talking about, lass?"

"The discussion we had before you teleported away. I followed up with Darius. As suspected, he took no souls of late. He tells the truth. Now I need you to do the same. Jack Macintyre: Have you taken any souls that might have belonged to Set?"

Jack paused. In theory he should be able to continue lying directly to them and they would not know the difference, but if there was one thing he had learned in his time here it was that he knew only a fraction of what was possible.

"Anything is possible, lass."

"A diplomatic dodge if I ever heard one." Mikon snorted. "And I heard many in my days as a Senator."

Crisa pushed the line of questioning further, however. "The attack on the docks. It seemed out of place at the time. It wasn't though, was it? You took those souls from Set and staged the attack, didn't you?"

Jack looked around the room. Each of the council members looked like they were ready to attack at the drop of the hat. Jack realized he had to tread carefully.

He reached out and did something he had hoped he would not have to do: he reviewed Darius's memories. Whether through habit or sloppiness, the group seemed to have forgotten that the man was directly connected to Jack. The review confirmed the worst of what he suspected. During his absence, Crisa had summoned the council and each had discussed events of the last several months. They had put many pieces together in a far more efficient manner than he would have thought they could have.

The council was a powder keg and he was dancing around with a lit torch.

"Aye. But here me out." He held up his hands as the group's grumbles began to grow.

"I needed ye all to be on your guard. I do plan to get us out of here. Back beyond the Glacier. But I canna do that with Set roaming about. There are no gods there anymore, not the way we are here. Nor should there be. I feel I can count on you all to do the right thing and free your souls when we break through, but not her."

"Do you think us, stupid, Jack Macintyre?" Golnar huffed. "If a way existed back across the Glacier we would have found it. Stop using fantasies as excuse for your betrayal."

"Set never attacked us, did she, Jack?" Crisa continued, with single minded persistence. "You set this entire power struggle up."

"We're close! You don't understand! I have a way back across the Glacier!"

Crisa ignored his plea and continued her cross examination. "And Darius? That wasn't her either, was it? You attacked one of our own. You put him at risk, stole his autonomy."

Jack could feel the pain and rage seeping through his link to Darius. He also realized that the group had come to a decision prior to his return on what they planned to do.

"You don't want to do this, lass. Give me time and I will free us. We really are close."

"No." Crisa shook her head. "I trusted you. I pushed your cause. I helped make you a god. And in doing so I share in your betrayal. Give me back the helm, Jack. I will take the mantle back upon myself until such time as someone more worthy steps up."

"Can't do that, lass."

"Don't make this worse, Jack. If you surrender peacefully your soul will be kept intact, as will those of your charges. We will allow you to live out as much time as you want in whatever manner you see fit. When you grow weary of this world we will see to it that you are each recycled into good lives. It is the best offer you will get."

"Not the best offer."

Jack felt his lines of power grow dark. One by one the energy conduits leading to the Helm went dark, until only his links to the souls he had directly established remained. Between his own crew, Darius, and the souls he had snatched in secret from the underworld he was still far more powerful than he would ever have even dreamed of back in the Prime, but even so he felt ridiculously weak compared to what he had been just a few seconds ago.

"This is your last chance, Jack Macintyre. You cannot hope to defeat us all. Hand over the helm willingly or your soul will be shattered into so many pieces that not a single one of us will be able to remember that you even existed at all."

Jack knew she wasn't bluffing. But he also knew that giving up his power now all but insured his link to the training Sanctuary and through it Thomas would be severed forever. Without it, even if Thomas was able to redo whatever it was that he had done to contact him before, it would likely not be enough. He, Huang, Jacob, and Heather would well and truly be trapped her forever.

He also knew that if he lost the helm then his chances of victory were over. As soon as the helm was back on Crisa's head the council would re-establish their links to it. The centralized power would amplify beyond anything he could hope to defend against.

"I am well and truly sorry, folks." Jack stated truthfully. "My intentions have always been pure, though my actions might not always seem so. They still are. I hope perhaps one day you can all forgive me."

Jack reached up to his head and grasped the helm, which materialized in his hand as he pulled it from his head. "But I told you, lass, that you really didn't want to do this."

Before anyone could react Jack pulled Darius's soul into his own. With it, all of its connected souls, and the ones Jack had stolen from the underworld it gave Jack a split second of action before any of his peers saw him move. With the speed of thought he summoned Huang and Heather in front of him and instructed them to not let anyone pass. A fraction of a thought later and Jacob appeared behind him, his black blade sucking the light out of the room.

As the horror of something behind out of place dawned on his peers, Jack tossed the helm over his shoulder towards Jacob. In one smooth motion the Angel of Death swung his dark blade forward, cleaving the ancient helm in two.

Screams of anger and outrage filled the room, with Crisa's voice being the most prominent. "What have you done?!"

"What I had to, lass. Only what I had to."

Chapter 33

Thomas gazed around in confusion, trying to determine what had happened. A moment ago he was talking to Jack. Now that link was gone and rather than their icy room, he now stood back in the realm of the Glacier. Well, he reassessed, not standing. Lying. He found himself now flat on his back. How had that happened?

He felt a sense of panic through his link with Buster, then resolution that was even more frightening. Buster was about to die. And it seemed to be his fault. His connection with the Glacier of Gods and Monsters had been severed and without it he had no connection to Jack but worse, Buster was helpless in a fight that could quite literally claim all of their souls.

A scream caught his ears and Thomas dragged himself away from Buster's fate long enough to determine his own. Shantae was on the ground, moaning. His energy level was so low that Thomas was reasonably certain that it was only her connection to him that kept her from dissipating. Cho was moving like lighting, striking a figure who didn't appear to be affected much more than someone dealing with a pesky fly that remained just out of reach.

"Coughlin."

The man looked over and smiled sadly at Thomas before reaching out and catching Cho by the throat as the small Asian man made another pass.

"Young Thomas. I apologize, but I warned you that if you stood in my way I would be forced to destroy you. I really did not wish to do that."

He let loose a charge of energy that staggered Thomas through his link to Cho. When Thomas was able to look up again, Cho too lay on the ground unmoving. Thomas could still feel the man through their link, but just barely.

Coughlin continued walking slowly towards him, ignoring Thomas's two compatriots as if they were already less than nothing to him. "I really hoped that you would see the way. I prayed over it every time you made a step against me. You are special, Thomas. I can see that. With you at my side we could have been the world's saviors, bringing forth the second coming at a far faster rate than I will be able to do on my own."

Thomas could feel the power radiating from the man as he closed in. But that power was little compared to the Glaciers around them. Thomas knew if he could re-establish his link, he could end this quickly. He shot backwards to his feet, grabbing a link from his shoulder as he did. He moved to send it towards the nearest Glacier...

And found himself lying on his back again instead.

"No Thomas. I do not know how you managed to do what I failed at, but I will not allow you to use that against me. I have let you live too long. Break your links to your companions and only you will need to die. I will let the others leave. If you do not, then all of them will perish with you. I will give you one minute to decide how many of them you will take with you."

Thomas ran through his options. He clearly stood no chance of regaining his connection to the Glacier. He still had the charged soul stone, but he had failed to get it transformed into a soul blade. That knife might have given him an edge, but that was clearly no option now.

Frantic, he burrowed into Senekay's memories. The man had always instructed him to do whatever it took to survive, so obviously he wouldn't object to the privacy invasion. What would he do in this situation? Thomas filtered the experience through Senekay's extensive memories in an attempt to find out.

And found one. With a flick on his wrist he produced the soul stone in his hand. He might not be able to use the souls within to create a blade, but he was thrilled to realize he could use it as a battery. A tiny version of the Glacier.

It was his only shot. Thomas crushed the stone in his hand, soaking the soul energy in as he did so. A rush of memories, many disturbing, started to flood into his mind, but Thomas wanted no part of them. He channeled the energy in the blink of an eye into a giant fireball and let it fly.

The speed caught Coughlin off guard, sending the man flying towards the River. Thomas knew it would not have the power to put the Preacher in, so he channeled some of the remaining excess energy into his two partners, bringing them back to their feet.

Coughlin stopped himself just a foot shy of the roiling River.

"Impressive Thomas. You are stronger than I gave you credit for. I won't make that mistake again."

Thomas mentally ordered his two companions to attack. They weren't fast enough. Before Thomas could even blink Coughlin shot towards them, seizing them by their throats. Thomas felt another double jolt of energy shoot through each and their links, the power of which dropped Thomas to his knees. He looked up just in time to see his two companions slamming towards him. Instinctively he let them pass through and into him, taking their energy for his own.

In their weakened state, they made little difference, and before he could move he found himself dangling, his feet kicking in the air, a steal vice around his own neck.

"I am sorry, Thomas, but I cannot allow you to end my quest like this. It truly is you or me. When God returns, I will ask that your soul be returned. For now, Good Bye."

Thomas braced himself for the shock that had rattled his two friends. For a brief second he wondered if he should cut his parents loose before it happened, saving them from this fate.

"Impossible."

Thomas realized his feet were back on the ground. He opened his eyes to see that Brother Parkes Coughlin still had his hand around his throat, but was staring at his other hand with a mix of anger, fear, and incredulation.

"No. No, this is not... Why?" He tossed Thomas to the side, seemingly with much less force than Thomas would have expected, then balled his fists and screamed at the sky "WHY?""

In that moment, Brother Parkes Coughlin was gone. Thomas didn't know why or how, but he knew it mattered little. Through his link he sensed that Buster was, somehow, still alive. But without the power of the Glacier that would not last long. Thomas reached in and grabbed yet another link, preparing to reconnect to that power.

Chapter 34

"**H**OW COULD YOU?"

Giovanni had expected a response like this. "Calm yourself, Brother Parkes. All is part of the plan."

Parkes was pacing in a way Giovanni had not seen him do in their century of work together.

"It was MY POWER. How could you steal it?"

"It was the Creator's power, Brother." Giovanni cautioned. "You were wielding it, but in doing so you were taking it in the wrong direction. I'm afraid I had to step in and put a stop to that."

"You..." Coughlin spat with a mix of rage and frustration. "You have not seen what I have, Giovanni. I did what was needed to keep the visions of our loss from coming true."

"Your loss, Brother. Not ours."

Coughlin stopped cold, his mind obviously working over the response. Slowly, he calmed, but his face grew darker. When he spoke again, it was with a cold calmness. "Exactly what do you mean by that statement?"

Giovanni weighed how much to tell Coughlin. He had been a good tool. Almost as good as the monk Merek had been. At least more patient. But like the monk, Coughlin could not fully understand the true end goal. He did not have the historical reference to appreciate what needed to be done. "I have had my own visions, Brother Coughlin. We always knew our goal might require sacrifices. Your failure does not lead to the goal's failure. In fact, you may no longer even have a part in the success or failure of our goal."

"You are saying that allowing Young Thomas to proceed will actually further our goal."

Giovanni nodded. "Yes. That is correct."

"No." Coughlin shook his head. "No, I do not believe this. There is simply no way to reconcile the visions I received with our ultimate victory. It is simply not possible unless..."

Coughlin stopped and raised an eyebrow, staring at Giovanni with a questioning look. The elder could tell that the younger brother was on the verge of understanding, but did not wish to believe the truth. It was better not to burn this bridge if he didn't have to.

"Calm yourself, Brother Coughlin. I have given you guidance for near a century now. Will you not trust my council now?"

"You have acted as my council, it is true." Brother Coughlin replied, his voice holding a noticeable tinge of distrust. "But now I must wonder, did we serve the same goal? By all of our time together, I must ask you, and I trust you will be honest with me: Do you seek to bring back the Creator?"

"I seek to bring back my God."

"A careful choice of words. Let me rephrase. Do you seek to bring back the same God that I do?"

Giovanni again weighed his words. He could lie, but Coughlin had a knack for discerning the truth of things, and Giovanni respected that. He had long been able to lead Coughlin foward with subtle hints that allowed the preacher to rely on his own conclusions. Blatantly lying was something all together different.

As it happened, he didn't have to.

Coughlin pulled himself up to his full height, growing noticeably colder in the process. "Your silence tells me that the answer is no. You have betrayed me all of this time, lead me astray. But you taught me much during that time. Our friendship ends here. Do not cross my path again."

With that final word, Coughlin disappeared. Giovanni considered bringing him back. He had the power to do so, but it mattered little at this point. The only way he would stop Coughlin would be to disperse him all together, and the man had earned more than that.

Besides, the goal was too far along for Coughlin to stop things now. Whether it was his scion or Ardru's made little difference. The results were all that mattered. He had waited centuries for this. Now that it was at hand, he cared little for anything Coughlin might choose to do.

His Lord was coming back. That was all that mattered now.

Chapter 35

Running Wolf dove out of the way of a massive paw swipe, letting loose another stream of arrows into the creature's side as he did. The creature had slowed dramatically from its original speed, but it remained a near blur. Running Wolf had to spend most of his time in defense, dodging and weaving around swipes that he feared would be powerful enough to dissipate him if they connected with their full force. He was still able to draw bits of energy from Thomas, but compared to the steady stream he had received this remained a trickle. Certainly not enough to sustain the levels of energy he expended.

Running Wolf dove once more over a low raking claw, raising his bow to again attempt to sting the Great Bear. The Bear had grown more cunning, however, and the rake suddenly altered course just enough to catch Running Wolf's midsection.

The force sent him flying and tore a massive amount of energy from his body. Running Wolf stood just in time to see the Bear charging directly at him. He let go of the energy required to keep his bow sustained and dove as far to the side as he could, spinning just barely out of the range of a massive bite.

"You will have me again soon, Great One."

It was a foregone conclusion at this point. Running Wolf's pride would not allow him to give in, but he could see the story play out. He no longer possessed the energy to attack the Bear. The best he could hope for would be to stay on the defense long enough to recharge as much of his energy as possible. Maybe, if he were near full amount before letting the creature take him, it might just be enough to allow Falling Dusk to regain control of himself.

Running Wolf dodged once again, barely getting grazed in the process. The odds of him keeping this up were falling. Either the Bear's speed was once again picking up, or Running Wolf's was falling. Perhaps it was both. The brave only knew that his very existence was starting to feel thin. If not for the link from Thomas, he felt certain he would have long since ceased to be.

"OVER HERE, MASTER!"

The voice was unexpected, as was the large spear that pierced the side of the Great Bear. "Come reclaim us!"

Running Wolf was relieved when the creature paused and turned away from him, allowing him to regain some of his energy. At the entrance to the large cavern, seven warriors appeared, each bearing the markings of a different tribe of old.

Running Wolf recognized the front one. It was Falling Sparrow, the brave he had met on his first reconnaissance to the area. They spread out quickly, each producing and throwing projectiles at the Bear. None of them seemed to be making much of a mark on the creature, but it none the less chased after them.

As a darker skinned female warrior took the creature's primary attention, Falling Sparrow slipped over to Running Wolf, helping him to his feet.

Running Wolf accepted the assistance with a nod. "Thank you, my brother."

"Do not thank us yet." Falling Sparrow replied grimly. " Our energy comes from the Great Spirit itself. We cannot change his levels, and so we cannot bring him out of this malaise. But he is near enough that I feel him. Within the Bear, the Great Spirit fights for control. He is allowing himself to be distracted by us. You, however, must give the final push."

Running Wolf nodded. "I will do what I can."

A scream behind them showed that the six warriors moving around the Great Bear had fallen to four. Those were holding their own, but their energy was visibly draining from them."

"That is all any of us can do." Falling Sparrow replied, then he created another spear and let it sail into the Great Spirit's side.

Running Wolf formed his bow. It took too much energy from him to do so, so he went back on the defense, yelling and hollering to draw just enough of the Bear's attention to keep it off balance with the other attackers. His energy was still being pulled naturally into the surrounding air, presumably by the Great Bear. That slowed his recharge rate to a disturbingly low level.

This was going to be close, he knew. Too close. But there was no escaping. At least he would fall with fellow Braves. As much as he appreciated Thomas and his group, being a part of a war party again, even if its prey was this deadly, soothed his soul in a way that he had not realized it needed. These were his people. If he fell at their side, it would be a good death. A noble death.

Thomas, however, must have had other plans. Just as Running Wolf began preparing himself for the end, his link exploded. Where he had ridden a fire-hose of energy before, now came a raging river.

Running Wolf transformed back into Buster just to burn off enough energy not to explode. With lightning fast reflexes he knew there was only one way to survive: dump the energy. The best way to do that was to charge once more into the Great Bear.

Again it sensed him, turning to give him a massive swipe, but he was faster than it now. Buster lept into the air, transforming once again into the tiny field mouse. The momentum carried him far over the swipe of the Bear, landing him on the creature's chest. He scurried around the side, transforming as he did back into the large German Shepherd and sinking his jaws deep into the creature. He then let go of all of the energy he could, turning himself into nothing more than a conduit for the massive power to transfer through his body and into the Bear's.

The power was too much too fast. Buster could not transfer it enough. He felt his very essence being burned away. Time ceased, and he could not tell what occurred from there.

Then, suddenly, his link snapped. Thomas was gone. He could no longer feel him or the massive power coming through. He could no longer feel anything. He stood in the presence of a blazing sun that blinded him to anything else that could exist.

Then, the sun turned to a gentle warmth as he felt himself collapse to the ground. A sense of safety he had not felt in centuries eased over him.

"Well done, young one. I'm proud of you."

Chapter 36

In retrospect, Jack would have done things differently. He wasn't sure what, but as he dodged and weaved his way around the Council of Hade's many and diverse attacks, he knew there had to have been some place along the line, some alternative choice he might have made, to have avoided this.

Maybe he could have brought more of the council in on his plan early? That seemed unlikely to have made a difference then, and seemed just as lacking now. Maybe he could have tricked more of them into giving him their connection the way Darius did? Again, unlikely. But the entire temple crashing around him made him want to believe there could have been a better path. Because this one's end sucked.

If he had been playing a video game, he would have reloaded by now. The Council had been worthy allies, and he did not want them as enemies, especially if he was now stuck for good on this side of the Glacier.

"Come now, good folks. Can't we talk this through?"

"You BETRAYED us, Jack." Crisa screamed, dropping gouts of fire at him in rapid succession. "You lied to us constantly. There is nothing left to talk about!"

Jack teleported away from the eruption of fire, barely spinning out of the way of a lightning bolt.

"I didn't tell you a few things, sure, but I've always tried to do what was best for everyone."

"YOU DESTROYED THE HELM!" Crisa screamed from behind him. Jack was glad for the heads up, as it allowed him to narrowly dodge her blow.

"Aye, well, you were going to use it against me, to be fair."

Destroying the Helm had not been something he had wanted to do. He had gathered all of the memories of its creation and knew its many strengths and weaknesses. It would have been far more useful to him against Set, but its destruction was the only reason he was still standing.

He held the advantage in power, the souls he had quietly gathered from the underworld combined with those that Jacob had reaped and all the ones connected to Darius meant he had more power than any of the Council standing ahead of him. They had also grown used to being able to draw on each other's powers when the need arose, which slowed their assaults considerably as they attempted to re-adjust to what they had access to.

Jack still had years of experience having to rely on merely his own power, the vast excess he could draw off of now gave him another leg up on what he would normally do. His cricket bat crackled with an energy that could shatter mountains, and easily deflected many of the more direct attacks lobbed his way.

The disadvantage was that he didn't want to actually take out these people, while they appeared more than eager to see him completely destroyed.

Jack considered his options. He had already scattered his team, warning them to lay low and prepare to be summoned . As of yet, they had not been targeted, but Jack would be surprised if that lasted. Were he leading the attack against himself, the first thing he would do would be to force the opponent to divide their resources. They had the numbers, so putting one of them each to tracking down Huang and Heather while leaving the rest to keep Jack busy would make him either pull the two in or spread his energy thinner.

Jacob was a wild card. Jack mentally reached out to his still half shadow companion.

"Jacob, lad. I need you to go Full Reaper."

"What? Are you crazy?"

"Aye, but that's not at issue here. The council's turned on us. If I send Heather or Huang into the fray, they'll be recognized. You still have the advantage of stealth. Poach every soul you can as rapidly as you can, else we're all finished."

He felt Jacob give a solemn compliance. The man hated what Jack had turned him into, and Jack hated having to do it, but both knew there was little choice in it. Their existence required these sacrifices.

Jack swung his Criket bat out, deflecting a ball of fire coming from Crisa at a swarm of arrows launched by Telekos. He then shifted his location again, keeping his opponents off guard as to where he was. He stayed close enough not to let them lose site of him. For now he held his own, but he suspected part of that was that they were all merely reacting, each attacking out of instinct. If they calmed down and started coordinating their attacks, he was going to have to change tactics to either take them out or fall himself. No other option seemed likely.

"Crisa, listen to me, lass, this isn't what we need to be doing. What if Set attacks?"

"All the more reason to end this quickly. If you truly cared about that, you would surrender now."

Jack couldn't do that, of course, but he also knew that this battle could only go on for so long. Like the battle against the Demon, it was a matter of attrition. They had the numbers, and in the end, if he didn't change that, they would eventually overpower him.

Suddenly, he felt a shift of something inside him. A faint connection. It wasn't fully there yet, but it was enough to give him hope. "Oh you incredible Lad. Jacob! Huang! Heather!" Jack screamed in his head. "To the Glacier!"

Jack then expended all of the energy Jacob had hastily gathered for him in a single burst. "ENOUGH!"

The burst was larger, than he anticipated. When it cleared, the entire temple was leveled, as was most of the surrounding city. The Council members hastily picked themselves up, growing visibly more angry as they looked around at the devastation surrounding them.

It was Mikon who spoke first. "Do you know how many centuries this city has stood? How much damage you have truly done?"

"Doesn't matter now, Lad."

"Does not matter to you, maybe." Katina spat. "You have not lived the lives we have. You have not seen the centuries float past. Were you to survive as long as we, your view point on such things would change."

"Change? Lass, I've seen every inch of this place. Change is the one thing lacking. You are stale. You live the same lives over and over and over, never adjusting, never creating. You exist, but only out of protest. That stubbornness was admirable when you had no alternative but to give yourself over to Set, but that's not longer the case."

"You would have us serve you instead?" Telekos spat. "A slave is a slave, no matter who their master is."

"Besides." Crisa added. "You expended far too much energy on that last stunt. You'll not be able to recover enough to stop all of us, even with this forced pause."

"Not going to need it, Lass. Nor do I plan to rule any of you. I'll even be letting Darius loose soon. There's a better way."

Intrigue. Offers of newness. After centuries of knowing virtually every secret in existence, it was the one thing the Council could not turn down. Jack watched as their collective guards lowered slightly. He just hoped it lasted long enough.

"What is it you plan, Jack?" Crisa asked. "Make it good and we might agree to reinstate our former offer."

Jack smiled. "Follow me, and you'll find out."

Jack shifted his position, suddenly finding himself standing with his back to the Glacier of Gods and Monsters. Huang, Heather, and Jacob all stood nearby.

"Dude." Heather commented as soon as he appeared. "What the hell did you do?"

Jack smiled and shook his head. "Hopefully bought us enough time."

"Time for what?" Huang asked quizzically.

"Time to go home, lad. Time to go home."

Chapter 37

Thomas felt power raging through him like a rampaging flood. There was no controlling it, very little directing it. The best he could do is keep it moving through the link to Buster where it exited as quickly as he could push it through.

To regain some semblance of control, Thomas expelled the souls of Cho and Shantae, ordering each of them to divert as much power as they could directly back into the River.

The two did so without question, though Thomas could feel that Shantae was struggling not to ask a number of things, and the tributary outlets they provided slowed the power down to an almost manageable level once more.

With the threat of being completely subsumed temporarily abated, Thomas once again traced the link from the Training Sanctuary back to Jack.

It was much harder to do this time for some reason, but after increasing the amount of power leading to it, Thomas was finally able to locate the other side.

"Jack! Jack are you there?"

"Thomas!" The voice on the other end sounded exhausted, and more than a little frantic. "Oh you incredible lad!"

"Sorry we got cut off earlier. Are you okay?"

"To be honest Lad, no. You remember that thing I told you to hold off trying earlier?"

"Blowing the Glacier?"

"Aye. Do it. Do it now if possible!"

Thomas considered. Senebkay's memories told him it was theoretically possible, but doing so would leave Buster cut off once more. That was unacceptable. "Can't just yet! But soon!"

"Aye then!" Jack replied with a mix of relief and exhaustion. "Very soon if possible. I'll do my best to stall!"

"Stall with what"?

But there was no response. Whatever Jack had gotten himself into was obviously taking his full attention to deal with. That concerned Thomas a bit, but at the same time, he knew if anyone could handle the impossible, it was Jack.

Suddenly a new voice entered his head. "It is done, Young One. Thank you."

The voice brought two revelations, one was that he recognized it from his dreams as the Great Spirit. The other was his link with Buster suddenly blinked out of existence.

The shock of losing Buster's connection was overwhelmed by the sudden mass of power building up inside him. Thomas had to find an outlet immediately. Luckily he already had that part figured out. With an exhausting effort of will power, Thomas shifted the flow of power from the Glacier through his connection in the Training Sanctuary, and through that back towards Jack.

A massive tidal way of Soul energy roared down the chosen pathway, hitting little resistance before suddenly stopping and building up. Thomas pushed more power foward, hoping to break through. It was the path or him, one would give and at this point he feared he might be the weaker of the two.

He redoubled his effort, forcing every ounce of the energy he could down the barely relenting pipeline. Every part of his being swelled with power, to the point where he started having to drain off excesses to everyone connected to him.

It wasn't working. His very soul was over expanding like a water balloon attached to a hose for far too long. He could feel himself faltering. For a brief moment he wondered what would happen if he let go. Would he actually explode? Would he take out all of those connected to him as well or set them free? Fear of the fate his friends and family might suffer held him tight, keeping him pushing forward, though it grew more and more painful to do so.

"Focus." A new voice, unbidden but again recognizable.

"Master Ardru?"

"Reach through your link. Find the weakness in the blockage. Redirect all power on that one point."

Thomas did so, fighting through the pain to trace the path he had sent the power through. It twisted through him, through the Sanctuary, back next to him, and up to the Glacier itself, very near the same spot he was drawing the power from to begin with. It was the Glacier that slowed the transfer back, its force keeping the link from expanding enough to take in the power of itself.

But the neaby link draining it created a weak spot, a place where the Glacier was starting to thin noticably. Thomas focused on that, pushing the power exiting the link to force the two points together. If he could just get them close enough, there was a chance it would....

The explosion threw Thomas to his back with a force that made Brother Coughlin's earlier attack seem gentle. It was only the rapidly draining excess power still coursing through his veins that kept him and his two nearby companions from being vaporized.

Thomas looked up to a spectacle he could not believe. Countless chunks of Glacier fell from the sky. None of them ever reached the River, each instead fell into a portal that opened beneath it then vanished without a trace.

Such portals had lead him to be born with Senebkays's powers. They had lead his daughter to be born with the soul of another goddess. Now there had to be a thousand pouring into the world.

"What have I done?"

"What you had to." Thomas looked up to see the Great Spirit walking up the beach next to him. To his great relief, Buster trotted next to him.

Thomas lept to his knees and gave the dog a hug. "Oh thank the gods you're safe."

Buster sat on his haunches, not seeming to object to the hug. "We did it. Thank you."

"It was a group effort, my friend." Thomas replied with a smile.

"Umm... I don't mean to interrupt." Shantae said, in a way that clearly meant to interrupt. "But is that what you intended to do?"

Thomas tuned away from his newly returned companion to see the full devastation he had wrought. Now that the portals had ceased opening, he could see that most of the Glacier remained, and many faint shapes peered out from it in either direction.

But in the center, where his link had been, a deep valley wound its way through. River essence, slightly faded somehow from its normal color, poured through at an increasingly rapid rate.

Thomas checked his link to Jack, and was met with news that brought both elation and horror.

"Yeah, that's what we wanted. But it might not have been what we should have done. Get ready. We're about to have visitors."

Chapter 38

Jack watched as, one by one, the remaining members of the Council of Hades appeared in front of him. Once all were in place, Crisa stepped forward.

"It's over Jack Macintyre. I do not know what foolish goal you thought to accomplish but it must end now."

"Almost lass." Jack knew his best bet was to keep them talking. The more they fought, the less energy they would have when Thomas completed his part of the plan. And he had no doubt that each of them would need as much energy as possible when that happened. "But don't you want to know why I have done all of this?"

"Does it matter?"

"Oh, aye. It matters a great deal lass. Humor me. I won't run. I'm right where I needed to be."

Crisa looked over her shoulder at the others. None seemed in a hurry to quickly re-engage in the fight. Jack realized that he must have drained them more than they let on when he destroyed the Helm. A good sign for him now, but not necessarily good if his plan played out.

Her cohorts not objecting, Crisa turned back to Jack with a shrug. "Fine. As condemned, you may have your final words. But know that your execution will not be long delayed."

"Oh trust me, lass. I've no interest in dragging this out long." Jack smiled. "But tell me, and humor me on this hypothetical. If I had been able to bring the wall down, would you have welcomed returning to the cycle of life and death?"

Crisa's face darkened. "There is no point in such hypotheticals, Jack Macintyre. Dreaming of the impossible only brings depression that can not be escaped."

"So you would, then?"

"Of course I would! We have roamed this land a thousand lifetimes beyond what any of us ever wanted. We have each been where you were, Jack Macintyre.

Wanting to go home, desperately wishing for the end. Many of the souls we took on were those that were far more powerful in strength than us, but they could not handle the crippling loneliness of eternity."

Crisa looked about sadly, nobody else among the group seemed willing to speak. "We have been where you are Jack. But hope only exists where there is a remote chance of something happening. There is no chance of going back to the other side of the Glacier. None. We have spent lifetimes looking for every possible scenario. It doesn't exist. Wishing for the impossible is a waste of time."

Jack felt something. A rumble in his connection with Thomas. Power began flowing into his veins, a trickle compared to the amount he already possessed but there was something right at the edge of his reach that radiated immensely more than he had even felt through the Helm.

"See, you lot are strong, aye, it's true. But you've spent life time after life time searching without the one thing you needed to achieve your goal."

Telekos stepped forward, obviously growing impatient with the discussion. "Tell us what that would be, Jack Macintyre. What is it that you, in your barely one life time's worth of experience, have that we with all of our lives between us are missing."

There it was. The power building, growing at the edges of Jack's connection. It was a slow motion nuclear explosion, and he was riding the edge of ground zero. It made Jack smile in a way that he knew Telekos would likely take as a defiant response to his question. And there was no reason in Jack's mind it shouldn't have been taken that way.

"Me mates. " He replied simply.

And then the Glacier of Gods and Monsters detonated. The massive explosion caught everyone off guard. Everyone except Jack. He felt an immense energy influx as a surge of power coursed through his link. Time slowed relative to the others, and Jack used that time wisely. In the blink of an eye he pulled Jacob, Huang, and Heather into him, sending them completely into the small room in his head. He also re-established Jacob's full body. They would no longer have a need for him to be hidden. Either they would return fully to the other side or they would all be completely vaporized. Either way, Jacob deserved to spend the end of this world as his fully formed self. Jack locked a few key memories away as well, things he knew might be of use if he somehow managed to survive this apocalypse. Then he unleashed the excess energy into one massive burst that sped its way forward towards the Egyptian lands, destroying every link to every soul it passed over.

Jack knew it wouldn't be much, but he hoped the energy expended would weaken Set if only by a little bit. He suspected every little ounce was going to have to count if they were to survive.

As time returned to full speed, the River that had made the Ocean began surging around and through them. Its undertow was too strong. Jack realized through his link that the entire world was quickly becoming unmade, each and every Sanctuary making it up began melting away, rushing back to the River that it longed to be a part of once again.

Jack didn't fight it. He gave in, falling backwards and riding the roaring rapids that wound its way through the Glacier itself. At first it was pure elation. He had done it. He was going home.

Slowly, a new problem began to emerge. The river he road rapidly became less diluted, more pure. The caucauphanie of sound he had heard so many times in other Sanctuaries began to roar once more, and his skin began to tingle.

As they rushed forward, the tingle became increasingly painful, and within moments he felt as though he were swimming in a river of acid. His skin boiled and burned and Jack felt his energy, the souls he had gathered from the other side, starting to be stripped away.

"So be it." He thought. He would protect the souls of his close friends for as long as possible, but if the others long stolen from the cycle of life and death were now to be returned, then truly so be it. If his was to be returned as well, that was at least preferable to the endless eternity of boredom that had awaited him just hours before.

As the acid grew more intense, Jack began to have second thoughts on his plan. He fought against the burning, trying to seal away the pain. Fading away into the River was one thing, but doing so in immense pain was an all together different fate. He tried his best not to make himself feel the souls being leeched out of every part of his skin that touched the current. He was able to lesson the horror but not fully end it.

Finally, as he felt his mind might be subsumed with madness to overcome the pain, a familiar voice rang out to him.

"Jack! Over here!"

Jack turned and stood, finding himself able to reach the bottom of the inlet he now floated in. In the distance, strangely smaller than he remembered, stood the source of the voice.

Thomas Salazar waved at him from the shoreline.

Chapter 39

Thomas had a mixture of elation and horror at the sight of a ten foot tall Jack come rushing in through the Valley of the Glacier.

Elation because the sight of his friend, whom he had once known he would never see again, was so joyful it almost made his heart burst. Horror because the pounding sense of deja vu accompanied the sight, and Thomas had vivid and disturbing flashbacks to the vision he had once held of himself as Senebkay destroying everyone he loved.

Events had obviously worked out slightly different from those that he had seen, but it created no less fear in him that if things went the wrong way here, everyone he loved could pay the price of his failure. He had to ensure that didn't happen.

The best way to do that, he decided, was to get Jack back on his side.

"Jack! Over here!"

The giant version of his old friend must have heard him. He stood up, the deep portions of the River only proving to be knee deep on him, then he slogged his way, wincing with every step, towards the edge where Thomas and the others stood.

There was a strange sense of nervousness coming from Shantae that he couldn't place. It was a mix of fear, excitement, love and other complex emotions intertwined. An odd enough sensation that Thomas had to push down his access to her link to keep from being distracted. Other figures were now emerging from the rift of the Glacier, equally tall figures dressed in strangely ancient clothing ranging from simple robes to ornate armor.

They seemed extremely confused and as in as much pain as Jack, who shrunk as he touched down on the shore to be more of his natural size.

"Oh lad, ye don't know how happy I am."

Thomas reached forward and gave his friend a giant hug. "Jack! I really didn't think I would ever see you again."

"Aye, well, ye have. And at least if things go too far south, I'll have been able to give you a proper goodbye."

Thomas didn't like the sound of that statement. "Those giants. Are we going to have to fight them?"

Jack looked over his shoulder. "Nay. I don't think so anyway. Been inside their heads enough to have a good read on them. They'll help us here in a moment, and likely sacrifice themselves doing it."

Thomas looked out at the giants walking towards Jack with looks that ranged from outright pain to determined grimaces.

"What do we have to fight then?"

The answer came with a ground shake. Thomas looked around for the source of the tremors, which suddenly began to become more pronounced and regular. Then he spotted the source. Leaping out over the edge of the glacier, a titanic figure from his memory crashed down, splashing River essence in waves around her.

"Her." Jack stated, nonchalantly as he pointed to the thirty foot tall Cleopatra. Thomas recoiled in horror as fresh memories of his vision appeared anew. Now all he needed was Brother Coughlin's demon and it would be the end of times for certain.

"Listen" Jack screamed at him. "If we don't stop her, she'll take the entirety of reality and remake it in her image, and there won't be a bloody thing any of us could do about it. "

He waved his hands and the three others that had disappeared with him when they fought against the Demon reappeared, seemingly frozen at the edge of the River. Jack then turned back to him. "For all of the power that you have gathered, you still won't last out there. Do your best to keep her busy from here. If I fall, these lot will wake and help you. But…" He smiled glancing at them, "they're too bloody stubborn for me to let go before that. They'd rush out to my side and get themselves melted for certain."

"Don't fall, Jack." Thomas wasn't sure he could lose his friend this soon again after getting him back.

"Be happy for me, lad." Jack replied, a tint of sadness to his voice. "I've had a good run, and if not for you I would have suffered a fate worse than this by far. We end this now. My fate's not important."

With that Jack turned, grew back to his enlarged size, and rushed back into the River. "Council! We MUST stop Set!"

To Thomas's surprise, the other giants turned their attention towards the titan, a figure that stood nearly twice the height of any of them, and charged forward.

Thomas felt a bump against his hand and turned to see Buster, with the Great Spirit standing next to him.

"Young one." The Great Spirit said placing a hand on his shoulder. "It seems the battle did not end with the God Monk. My people are once again needed."

"That includes me." Buster added.

"No." Thomas shook his head, realizing what they were saying. "No, Buster. I need you."

"You do not. You are a capable chief. Lead your people well. I thank you for your friendship, but my people need me at their side. I gave my soul for this. It is a thousand summers past the time that it should have been collected."

Thomas knew there would be no talking him out of it. And in the back of his mind he realized it wouldn't have been fair to try. He selfishly wanted to keep his best friend in life and death at his side, but it was only for his selfish reasons, not for Buster's needs. Buster, or Running Wolf as he had been known to his people, had a deep sense of duty. Thomas knew keeping him out of this fight would only bring his loyal companion a deep sense of shame that would last all his days. Thomas could not wish that on him.

With tears streaming down his face, he nodded his assent to his friend. That was all the dog appeared to be waiting for. He turned stepping into the Great Spirit. The Great Spirit then nodded to him as well, pivoted, and began charging out into the River. As he did, his form changed to that of a massive bear. Its size rivaled that of the giants, though it remained a good bit smaller than the titan.

Thomas turned to Cho and Shantae.

"We can't join them. But that doesn't mean we can't help. Throw everything you possibly have at her."

Chapter 40

"You fools!" Set hissed, her voice booming through the valley. "Why fight me now? Look around you! The Gods are all dead, trapped in this nightmarish ice. We can rule now!"

"No" Mikon replied, sending a whirlwind of River spray crashing into the giant Egyptian. "Our time is over. We can sleep now."

Set elbowed Mikon and Golnar to the side, then sped forward with incredible speed to seize the old Senator Mikon by the throat. "If you want to sleep, then do it. But you will not take me with you!"

Jack assessed the situation. Crisa, Katina, Telekos and Golnar were attacking with a fury he'd not seen them unleash even on him. Mikon quickly picked himself back up and rejoined the fray. Their attacks were landing, but every one drained their own levels as quickly as it drained Set's and she seemed to have exponentially more power than even the large group of them combined. The large bear crashing towards them would improve the odds, but Jack didn't think it would overturn them.

From the sidelines, Thomas, Cho, and some woman connected to Thomas unleashed a combined torrent of fireballs, arrows, and gunfire. They hit their mark but were little better than mosquito bites.

Jack blocked a swarm of insects rushing towards him with his cricket bat, splattering what he could with River essense. The resulting splash took out the insects but also ilicited a scream from Golnar as it covered her in its acidic touch.

The giant bear rushed in, throwing its great weight at Set. She managed to dive out of the way of the full force, but the great beast's claw reached out and grabbed her as it flew by, raking across her skin and sending her flying backwards into the River. The resulting cannon ball sent waves of fire flying fifty foot into the air, raining pain on everyone nearby.

"This isn't working!" Crisa cried out. "We're hurting ourselves more than we're hurting her."

"We've no choice, lass!" Jack screamed back. "We let her get to land and she could start drawing in other souls to replenish herself. This is our only hope of stopping her."

"No." Crisa replied, stepping close to him. "It's not our only hope. Or even our best one."

She looked over as Set began swinging the Great Bear away from her, using its mass to carry it back off deeper into the River.

Crisa placed a hand on Jack's shoulder. "Power is exponential. We'll never defeat her spread out like this. I'm tired of this fight. You were the last Hades. Finish this."

Before Jack could comment he felt her.. melt into him. That was the best he could describe it. One moment she was in front, the next she became part of him, her power joining and expanding his, her memories threatening to overwhelm his own.

Jack reclaimed himself, using the tricks he had learned on the other side of the glacier to lock her away deep in his own mind.

He turned in time to see Mikon rush towards him. He thought for a moment the old Senator was going to attack him for what Golnar did, but then he realized that the man was doing the same. Within seconds Jack felt his power grow again.

"No!" Set roared behind him. "This world will be mine! I will not allow you to stop me!" She turned to rush him but was attacked from behind by the Bear, who despite his smaller size and power base fought with a tenacity that forced Set to give it her full attention.

Jack realized he too was surrounded. The remaining council members were ignoring Set and focused completely on him.

Golnar gave him a mischivieous smile. "Hades's will be done." Then she and the remaining members all merged into him as well.

Jack took their power, locking the memories together into the island hut in his head. He looked over to find himself significantly closer to Set's size, though still noticably smaller.

Jack moved with lightning speed, swinging his tower sized club into Set's back. The woman shifted, sending a barreling attack by the Bear wide, forcing the beast to crash near Jack, splashing him again with acidic River essence that burned away more souls.

Jack moved as if his life depended on it, and the Bear put on an impressive show, but Set had obvious experience in these fights. The two on one should have over powered her, but at best they were all diminishing at a near equal pace.

The River was getting deeper as Jack's height melted away, and the deeper it became the more rapidly he felt his power melt.

For her part, Set shrunk too, but still appeared far more powerful than anyone else nearby.

Jack realized there was a chance they might lose this. His best bet, from all evidence, was to keep it close enough that when Set finally destroyed them there was increased odds of Thomas and his group overpowering her.

That was a long shot. Jack remembered how much trouble they had had with the Demon, and it couldn't have been more than just a handful of souls. Set likely still had thousands at her disposal, and at this rate might have at least hundreds by the time he exhausted his supply.

He was attempting to figure out an alternative plan when he felt someone else grab him. Jack turned his head in surprise as he felt himself get lifted up.

The new figure did not fill him with hope. "Argos."

"Finally" Set shouted. "Deal with that insolent whelp. I'll deal with the Beast."

Jack's heart sank. "You can't do this lad."

"I can do things you have never thought of." Argos replied. "Like take back my friends."

Jack screamed as he felt the cottage in his mind forcefully ripped away. Along with it, the power that had been given him by the others drained rapidly through Argos's grip. Even Darrius' power slipped away from him, and with it the few remaining souls from the Underworld.

In a matter of moments, Jack realized that the only soul within him was his own. He had shrunk back to his original size, while Argos had grown in stature as he had in power. Jack was little more than a rag doll, with about as much control over his fate.

"You freed our souls." Argos boomed, staring at him with his massive face only a few feet away. "For that I will spare yours."

Jack suddenly felt himself launched through the air. The world a blur of motion, before coming to a sudden stop in what Jack quickly realized was some form of giant pillow that Thomas must have no doubt created to cushion his fall.

Jack bounced up, much slower than he felt he should have, just in time to see a much smaller version of the giant bear crash into an other pillow near by.

"Thanks for the save, Thomas, me lad, but you might not have bothered." Jack pointed out at where Set stood, still massive in size, with a slightly larger Argos wrapping his arms gently around her waste. "We are well and truly screwed."

"People of this land!" Set's voice boomed. "We are your gods now. You will bow before us or be destroyed."

"No."

To Jack's surprise, it was Argos who dissented.

"The world of gods has passed. It is time we do as well."

Before Set could react, Jack saw Argos pick her up, then fall backwards into the River while clasping her close.

Furious kicks and movement erupted with geyser like splashes of River from the place where they disappeared. Then, after minutes of everyone staring on, a rapid flash of portals suddenly appeared and disappeared over the spot.

After that, silence. Jack looked around. His crew, Thomas's bunch, and the bear all stood at the River's edge. Silence was only disturbed by the dull noise the River made this close to the Glacier. Nobody seemed ready to move or believe it was over.

Finally Jack couldn't take it. "Well I'll be damned. He did the right thing." He shook his head then turned to the others. "Let's go back the Training Sanctuary. I need a recharge."

Chapter 41

"Jack! My Friend!" Leo exclaimed as he rushed up to meet him. It was rare for Leo to leave his own sanctuary, but Thomas understood why he would have done so now. "It is good to be seeing you!"

Jack wrapped the energetic Italian into a great bear hug. "Good to be seen, mate. Gods it's good to be seen back here." He stepped back, and his eyes grew a bit sad. "Thomas told me about Charlotte. Hell of a loss. I'm proud of you for keeping things going."

"The credit," Leo smiled, "does not go to me. You chose well with Thomas and Cho. They have done well."

Thomas smiled. "Just tried to do what we thought you would."

He looked over the other direction to see Shantae approaching Jacob carefully, a sense of awe radiating from her link. "It's..." tears started to flow down her cheeks. "it's really you. I... I just... Just don't believe it."

From what Thomas had heard of the man, he expected Jacob to push away, but instead an uncomfortable look of confusion crossed his face. "I'm sorry, I feel like I know you but..."

"Oh." A smile crossed Shantae's face and she nervously pushed her hair back over her ear. Thomas could tell by the way she awkwardly kept looking between Jacob and the ground that there was something between them. "I guess I do look a little different. Maybe this will help."

With a smile, Shantae returned to the form Thomas had only seen her use once, back in the Church where he had first recruited her. It was obviously not the first time Jacob had seen it though.

"Marcus?!" Thomas was more than a little surprised to see Jacob pick the smaller man up and pull him close. That surprise faded quickly as he realized from the emotions freely flowing out of Marcus's link that the two had been lovers in life, separated by Jacob's untimely death. Thomas had to admit a pang of jealousy as he considered what it would be like when his beloved Shari finally joined him.

"Oh Marcus, man, what the hell are you doing here?"

"Died, man. Then your boy Thomas over there brought me into his group. I've been helping out ever since. Oh, it's so good to see you!"

Heather bounced over to the two. "You must be someone pretty special. I've never seen Jacob light up like this."

Jacob cast her a sideways glance. "Play nice, Red."

Heather laughed and extended her hand. "To you? Never, but to your friend, well I'm Heather, Jacob's big sister on this side of death. Anybody that can produce a smile like that on Jacob has to be worth knowing."

Thomas let the group continue with their banter, and turned back to where the Great Spirit and Buster were talking and walked over. "So. What now?"

The old Medicine Man smiled. "Some of my remaining souls would like to check in on their people. I will take them. Then we will return to the Creator. We have earned a rest."

Thomas turned to Buster, afraid to ask the question on his tongue, but more afraid not to. "What about you, old friend?"

Buster looked back and forth between Thomas and Falling Dusk. Thomas could tell the decision was not an easy one for him. The Medicine Man must have as well.

"You fought bravely, Wolf." The old native told him. "You did your people proud. But now our fight is over. His continues. If you are not yet ready to rest, I have no doubt you would be of great use here."

The dog sat on his haunches and nodded. "I will stay. Thank you, Great Spirit."

Falling Dusk turned back to Thomas and extended his arm. "Our paths will not cross again. I do not know where your passage will lead you. You have done a great service to me and my people. I wish you well on your remaining journey."

"Thank you." Thomas nodded, clasping the old man's arm. "I hope you find what you are looking for."

The Medicine Man bent down and whispered a final message to Buster, then turned and disappeared. Thomas was lost in thoughts about the man and his journey when Jack walked up to him and handed him a strange looking helmet.

Thomas took it and turned it over, looking at it. "What's this?"

"A helm." Jack smiled. "Based on something I discovered on the other side. We don't want to risk accidentally becoming what we fight against. I think it's time you and I turned loose of the souls connected to us. But..."

"But Brother Coughlin is still out there. And maybe others like him."

"Indeed, lad. This is the answer. Saved the memories of how to make it. It'll let us link our people to it instead of us. They can choose to loan us their power, and it will protect them from being taken against their will. But it leaves control with them. They can sever the link whenever they choose."

Thomas looked at the helm again. "Good. I'm tired of being a Greater Spirit."

"Don't get too tired. Somebody's still got to wear the bloody thing."

Thomas tried to hand it back. "That should be you."

"No lad." Jack shook his head, pushing the helm back. "I'll show you how it works and help you make everyone's connections, but I'm through being a bloody god. You've no idea what I've gone through. I need a break."

Thomas sighed. He had thought that by Jack coming back, things would go back to the way they had been. He supposed that some things can't truly go back. "Fine. But let's not worry about this now." He produced an ice cold mug of hard cider, then passed it over. "We need to properly celebrate your return first."

Jack took the proferred mug and held it up as a toast.

"Don't have to tell me twice, lad."

Chapter 42

B rother Giovanni looked out over the newly deformed Glacier, attempting to remember all of the Greater Souls that were no longer visible behind its icy mountains. Some he could place, others he wasn't certain about. The two that mattered, however, were definitely gone.

He felt the presence of his once opponent, who long ago turned into a friend. There were very few who knew what it was like to live through so many centuries. It naturally tended to create a bond.

"My congratulations, Ardru. You were successful."

The old monk stopped next to him, surveying the change himself. "We were successful."

"True. Who would have guessed it took the two of us working both together and in opposition to achieve our goal."

"Do you still think this was the right path?"

Giovanni shrugged. "Most of the gods still slumber. I think our Masters will be fine risking the return of the few others in exchange for their own freedom. You? You okay with this?"

Ardru nodded. "Somewhere out there, my Master draws breath for the first time in centuries. In time, he will remember his past and return to me. There is little that would not be worth that."

Giovanni hoped for the same. But it disturbed him somewhat that he could no longer read what the future might hold. For now, there were far too many possibilities. He hoped his own master would forgive him for his part in breaking him out of the hell that was The Glacier. All he could do now was wait and watch.

Here ends the Glacial Trilogy.

Note from the Author

I'm both honored and astounded at the feedback I have received from this series. Thank you all.

I've been writing for most of my life, and making up and telling stories even longer than I could put them on paper. In elementary school I was put by my teachers into a UIL style contest where I would hear a story, then have to retell it. I often advanced, though never actually won, often for the same reason: I never actually told the story back as it was, but was always able to fill in great details to make a new and different story.

Story telling stuck with me, and much of my college time was geared in one way or another towards sharpening my craft. I took classes in poetry, journalism, short fiction, long fiction, and screen writing for TV, Movies, and even advertising. All of it required different formats but all was at its best when you were telling a good story. When I graduated, I continued writing. I tried a few times to go the traditional publishing route, but lacked the patience required to go through all of the hoops. I love to write. I disliked sending out countless copies to endless publishers. I didn't care so much about the rejections, but did get annoyed at the games where you were expected to send one copy out to a group but not to others until you got that rejection.

In the end, I just wrote and shared my stories with my friends and family. They enjoyed it, and I enjoyed writing them. And that, for many years, was that. Then, a couple of things happened. First, I wrote a short story that my wife found exceptionally intriguing. It was an idea I had been working on for some time, combining many years of mythology studies with some random "what ifs" into the story of a man who found out that the afterworld was more complex than he ever expected. She asked if I would turn the short story into a novel, and after thinking about it, I realized there was a lot more to that story that wanted to be told. Thus was born "Waking Up Dead".

Around this same time, several other author friends of mine were starting to do well in Self Publishing. I realized, the tools now existed for me to do my own books, without having to go through all of the hoops of traditional publishing. So I wrote, rewrote, polished, and found a graphic artist friend to make a cover for my book and put it out there.

The results have far exceeded my expectations. I have received a number of wonderful reviews, and have had countless people track me down personally to tell me how much they enjoyed the books, and to ask (sometimes very insistently) when the next story would come out. This has driven me to write more, and, I hope, continue to make a better product.

This is the close of the first trilogy, but definitely not the end of my writing books. I've got more tales in my head than I'll likely ever have time to write, but I plan to get as many of them out there as I can. I hope you continue to enjoy them.

If you've made it this far, I have one favor to ask - Leave a review. I love having those of you who have met me in person tell me your thoughts, but telling others through reviews helps to spread the word, which helps me get more books out to you. Amazon, B&N, iTunes, Kobo, or wherever else you care to doesn't matter. Any review helps.

Thank you all, for your support. It means a lot.

- Zabe

About the Author

Zabe Truesdell is a writer, traveler, and explorer forced to work in the corporate world to pay his bills.